PRAISE FOR KAREN KROSSING'S
TAKE THE STAIRS

"Krossing's significant achievement is to create an utterly believable, complex teen world. The writing is strong and the characters are well-drawn. The crises are real issues facing many teens: abuse, unwanted pregnancy, fitting in, and homosexuality. *Take the Stairs* will appeal both to teens experiencing any of these problems and to parents who want to support them."

Quill & Quire

"An excellent collection... Not only does Krossing create a strong cast of characters, but she skilfully casts the Building as the 14th major character, one whose stairs lead out as well as in. Highly recommended."

Canadian Book Review Annual

"Through reading *Take the Stairs*, one develops a greater appreciation for the commonality that runs through people's lives: suffering, struggle and hope. These are not the glossy stories one sees on TV but the real lives of teens growing up in Canada in the twenty-first century."

Resource Links

"Krossing incorporates a remarkable range...each account resonates with the turbulent emotions of young people coping with the gamut of teenage issues."

CM Magazine

"The teenagers are appealing and realistic, sometimes troubled by life, sometimes hopeful, sometimes gaining their dreams. A thought-provoking novel and also a very good read. Highly recommended."

Hi-Rise

"In all of the stories, the teens cope in the best way they know how with the difficult circumstances that life has dealt them. Despite the challenges the teens face, there is a ray of hope that threads itself throughout the stories and keeps the reader intrigued."

KLIATT Review

PURE

PURE

KAREN KROSSING

Second
Story
Press

Library and Archives Canada Cataloguing in Publication

Krossing, Karen, 1965-
Pure / by Karen Krossing.

ISBN 1-896764-96-7

I. Title.

PS8571.R776P87 2005   jC813'.6   C2005-904202-8

Edited by Kathryn Cole
Copyedited by Sandra Braun
Front cover design by Karen Kraven and Laura McCurdy
Text design by Melissa Kaita

Printed and bound in Canada

Quotation on page 9 from *Anthem* by Leonard Cohen

*Second Story Press gratefully acknowledges the support of the Ontario
Arts Council and the Canada Council for the Arts for our publishing
program. We acknowledge the financial support of the Government of
Canada through the Book Publishing Industry Development Program.*

ONTARIO ARTS COUNCIL
CONSEIL DES ARTS DE L'ONTARIO

Canada Council   Conseil des Arts
for the Arts   du Canada

Published by
SECOND STORY PRESS
20 Maud Street, Suite 401
Toronto, Ontario, Canada
M5V 2M5

www.secondstorypress.ca

For Kevin, Paige, and Tess

*"There is a crack in everything.
That's how the light gets in."*
-Leonard Cohen

the portrait

The swarm of off-duty workers blasted apart, making way for two Purity guards. Like the shiver running across my skin, the guards' silver uniforms sent a rippling chill through the crowd. Anyone could be picked up by Purity, pure or not, and even questioning could become painful. These guards were walking their usual lakeside patrol, as if bio-invaders might bubble up from the lake bottom, spraying hazardous DNA molecules over everyone in Dawn.

Dawn. A promising name for a settlement. Purity loves names with promise, but Dawn only holds promise for some.

Dawn is a mind-numbing city surrounded by acres of boreal forest. There's a lake, a waterfall over the rocky cliff, our precious hydro unit, and lots of wholesome human DNA. We've got a fence to protect us from those bizarre creations in the Beyond. We're merely one link in the chain of Purity's controlled communities across the globe. *Pure forever. Protect the gene pool. Stake a claim in the New Canadian North.* With noble mottos, Purity hangs over us like an ominous spider ready to strike anyone who can't prove they're pure, unaltered DNA. And I was only another stupid fly caught in their web.

At the lakeside commons, I was foolishly trying to sell portraits to a crowd preoccupied with the size of our energy allowance, DNA registrations, and where to get the latest temporary IQ boost. No surprise that my portrait chair stood horribly empty. Rivers of people rushed past, splitting into two streams to avoid where I sat. In the large stone courtyard surrounded by unused benches and ignored gardens, who cared about a teen artist?

Heat shimmered above the rocks and skinny fir trees that crowded the lake. My feet steamed in my sandals, and my sunblock was fighting the usual battle. A kid on jet blades wove through the crowd. Everyone hurried past like they'd rather risk the Beyond than stop for a portrait.

Just snag someone, I thought.

I stood, stepping in front of a thin man dressed in the loose-fitting overalls of a greenhouse worker.

"Like a portrait?" I gripped my slate tighter.

He stopped abruptly, now a rock in the stream. People pushed around us, glaring. In his bony hand he held the leash of a transgenic animal — part monkey, part cat, I guessed. For Purity, gen-eng of animals and plants was fine, but don't touch human DNA. The man looked at me, then at my solar sign.

My sign stood on a flat of gray rock, catching the morning sun. PORTRAITS BY LENNI HANNIX — 1 CREDIT flashed in lights across the top of the sign. A modest price, I'd thought. I avoided looking at my sample sketches, parading across the bottom. Somehow, they'd never captured the images that were in my mind.

Would he like my sketches? I held my breath. Sweat trickled down my neck, creeping closer to my tanktop. I'd worn my hair in two braids to keep the thick mess off me, but it was no help. *Hurry up, old man.*

His beast scampered closer, hissing at my toes. Pointed teeth and glow-in-the-dark eyes. I jerked my foot back, leaving my sandal behind. Purity shouldn't allow those things.

The man frowned. "She just wants to meet you!"

"Sorry, I'm . . ."

He tugged the leash and strode around me. The animal scurried after him. Last I saw, it had climbed up his leg and was sitting on his shoulder, staring back at me with accusing eyes, as though *I* were the mutant.

I slipped my sandal back on and sighed. Maybe I shouldn't charge anything. Maybe I should offer pet portraits.

A brief pine-scented breeze off the lake cooled me then left me sweating again. I glanced up at the too-hot late-November sun, then returned to watch the rush of people weaving around me, across the courtyard, between the trees, along the walk. I noticed the jagged leaves of lifewort — the gen-eng plant my father's company had created — growing out of tiny crevices in the concrete. Lifeweed, the reporters now called it, although Dad still called it lifewort. I didn't know what to call it. Across from the commons, the shops and cafés were bustling, too. Beyond them were the towers of Center Block. Maybe I should set up there.

Then a middle-aged couple with matching gray hair cut short around their ears paused near me, glancing at my sign. I pounced.

"Like a portrait?"

"What for?" the man grumped. His eyes found my breasts then traveled slowly to my legs. I squirmed. I was the sort of person that most men looked at twice, and I hated it. I mean, I liked Jonah's eyes on me, but who wanted to attract a creep? The woman squinted and pursed her lips, reminding me of Mother. Gutter gypsies, Mother called street vendors. She stepped around them in distaste. Mother better not find me here.

"To remember . . . uh . . . this moment in your lives?" *Or to capture your scowl.*

"Humph."

The woman glanced at me accusingly then yanked her leering man away.

Butterfly wings began to stir my stomach. I should pack up. I wasn't a real artist. No one wanted a portrait. Oh, Mur, why was I doing this?

Then I remembered. Last night, Mur had whispered into my dream. *Draw portraits by the water.*

Mur was my childish slur of the word *mother*. I'd named her when I was just learning to speak, when I'd mistaken Mur for Mother. I was lying in my crib on my back, playing with my toes. Sunlight shone through the leaves outside, burst through the window to where I lay, and made the shadows dance. In that lick of sun and shadow, I played contentedly, until a pain in my belly made me cry out. It was probably hunger, but I didn't have a name for it then. I whimpered and wailed, pulled myself up and clung to the bedrail, calling for someone to sooth me. Yet no one came. I suppose Mother had been in some crisis then, but I had no way of knowing why I'd been abandoned.

Then I saw her.

She was standing over me, and the light and shadow leapt over her silver hair, her earth-dark eyes. When she spoke, a breath of wind stirred, scented with the rich promise of new spring growth. *Shh. All is well.*

Her voice was so soothing that the pain in my stomach vanished.

Mur, I cooed, naming her. *Mur.*

Mur was my dream spirit, my inspiration, my muse. I didn't know why she came to me or why I alone could hear her. I'd just always known her, and I couldn't draw without her.

In my dream last night, Mur had shown me the stylus gliding smoothly across my slate. People had lined up for one of my pictures. I'd made them laugh, smile, cry. This was nothing like my dream.

Then the chill returned to the crowd. The Purity guards were zigzagging back, searching each face carefully, stopping one terrified woman to quiz her. This wasn't regular patrol. Were they looking for someone? I held my breath and examined my toes. Drawing portraits was too public. What had I been thinking?

When I raised my head again they were gone. Enough. I didn't want Purity's attention, and offering portraits just might be considered strange enough for a closer look. I was embarrassing myself anyway. I folded one chair. As I reached for the other, a large woman in a billowing dress as dull as gray pixels waddled toward me. Before I could fold my second chair, she had squeezed herself into it, elbows pushed out to the sides and hands on the armrests.

"Are you any good?" she wheezed.

"I guess so." *Get out of here,* I thought. Yet this would be my first real portrait. I unfolded my chair and sat with a thump.

The woman leaned close enough for me to smell her sour breath. "What does that mean?"

I waved a hand at my sign. "See for yourself."

Without meaning to, I caught a glimpse of the sketch that was now showing. Myself with my parents. I'd sketched them from memory so they wouldn't have to know. It was hardly a success — too boringly realistic. I soared above them like a young willow tree while they were squat evergreens with wide behinds. We were so different. I used to pretend that I was adopted, although I knew I wasn't. My DNA registration clearly showed who my parents were.

"Good." The woman dropped a credit into my hand.

Good! I pocketed the credit. My hand trembled as I touched my stylus to my slate to power it. The slate was rechargeable, but I couldn't use up too much of my energy allowance.

Trying to concentrate, I stared hard at the woman's face. Small eyes, thin lips pointing down, deep creases on her forehead. Worst of all were the red-brown sunspots on her neck and the backs of her hands. Scaly, cancerous welts. I shrank back.

"Why aren't you drawing? I paid my credit."

"I am. I will," I stuttered.

Ignore the welts. I shut my eyes to capture what I would draw. Usually, I got the outline that way, then the details came as I sketched.

Nothing came.

Calm down, I thought. *You can do this.*

I swallowed hard to clear the lump in my throat. My heart raced. I could feel sweat gathering between my breasts.

Mur? Are you there?

Always. Mur's breath was earthy. Her hair was silver cloud.

Where is this woman? I can't find her portrait.

Let go.

Mur was before me, around me, within me. *Relax.* My jaw unlocked, muscles slackened. I searched for a way into the portrait, until my thoughts extended like fingers into the gray woman. Unexpected. Vile. Pull back. Too close to this stranger – to the slow, sluggish sense of her. As if her cells were covered with oil.

Then the image of what I was to draw invaded like a sickness. Thick, rancid oil began to choke me, to clog my throat with the stench of decay. I gagged. Struggled to hold onto myself, to plant firm in this oily smear, to bring a touch of life to the decay, like lifewort growing out of concrete.

When I opened my eyes, I gasped in the muggy air. My blood pulsed through my head with dizzying speed. The drawing was finished. How had I sketched with my eyes closed?

I gazed dumbly at what I'd drawn, still breathing hard. The vast landscape of the woman was a melting ooze. Her fingers dripped like grease toward the ground, her eyes stretched like two fried eggs. She was collapsed over the back of the chair as if her backbone were rubber. Yet a tiny stem of green had sprouted between the blobs of her toes.

The woman pulled the slate down so she could see her portrait. "That doesn't look a bit like me!"

"No, it doesn't." My voice so quiet it hid the tremble. None of my sketches were like this. So abstract. So confused. Yet so right. *Mur, what happened?*

Only what should happen.

My cheeks felt flushed and my palms were slick with sweat. I touched a spot on my slate to bank the image and another to transmit it to the woman's slate. The drawing looked nothing like her, but it was her somehow – except for the green stem. That was my own touch.

The woman's hand, gripping the side of my slate, had white knuckles. The bubbling welts of the sunspots were gone! Gone from her neck, too. Smoothed over into darkened patches of skin.

"Your hand!" I touched the spot. Satin soft. How?

She pulled back her hand as if I'd burned her. "How did you . . . ?"

"I . . . uh," I mumbled. The pounding of my blood was growing stronger, hammering in my ears like crashing waves. The green sprout. Could I have . . . ? Impossible!

"What are you?" The woman's eyes narrowed. "Are you skidge?" She stood.

Her voice pushed at me. Too loud. My head was throbbing. "Of course not!"

How dare she? I was no illegal genetic experiment. My registration proved it. I had full reproductive classification. I was pure. I hadn't even had an IQ boost.

"Purity will be after you!" The woman pointed at me.

I stood, arms on hips. People stared at us. The woman began to back away, still waggling one finger at me. I glared at her, willing her to stop pointing. Others were listening. The Purity guards might still be nearby. What if they believed her? I had nothing to hide, but Purity had a habit of investigating any unusual behavior.

"I'm pure!" I shouted, sounding like a desperate skidge. Really believable.

She crashed into my display sign and gave me one last accusing glance, not even waiting for a transmit of her portrait. My sign teetered on the rock for a moment, then righted itself.

The throbbing overtook me then, thumping steadily in my ears. I wanted to collapse back into my chair, to wait for it to slow. But fear of Purity picking me up, even for questioning, forced me to pack up and get out of there, head down, and walking as fast as I could manage.

skidge

When uniforms matter more than art, when everyone has the same haircut, you don't go and distinguish yourself by drawing portraits in the commons. Stupid. Why was I so stupid?

I stumbled into Nature's Way Café, my folded chairs slapping against my leg, the strap of my heavy bag cutting into my shoulder. All the tables were filled, but Jonah wasn't there. He'd promised to meet me. Where was he?

Cool indoor air, finally. Behind the long counter, the grill spat out the scent of fried vegetables and grease. I hauled my load through the tangle of tables, avoiding eye contact with anyone, and burst out into the sweltering heat of the side patio.

Too hot, but empty, except for one guy about my age, dressed in medic clothes, hunched over a game screen, his fingers plugged into the controls. Probably a medic trainee off-shift.

I weaved between clusters of tables and large shade trees, dumped everything in a corner, and slumped into a chair. The medic looked harmless enough. The fence around the patio made it mostly private. No one should notice us. *Hurry up, Jonah,* I thought. I needed to make sense of what had happened, and he always knew how to help.

The molded plastic chair trapped the heat against my skin. I rubbed at the ache in my shoulder. Mur's energy was gone, and my head still pounded slightly.

A skinny waiter entered the patio with a tall glass of pink juice on his tray. He was dressed in uniform, too – slate-gray shirt and shorts with a modest white stripe down each side. His hair was cut in the usual blunt unisex style. My own Academy uniform was stuffed deep into my bag. No one needed to know where I belonged.

I signaled the waiter over. Just then, the medic with the game screamed, as if he were being tortured. "Ahhhhh!"

I jumped, my bare legs peeling painfully off the chair with a ripping sound. The waiter almost spilled the drink.

"You all right?" he asked the medic.

My legs stung. I glared at the medic. Fool game junky. Must be playing Blass – a complex puzzle game. Everyone knew that you could damage the nerves in your fingers with that game.

The medic had bulky shoulders. His arms rippled with muscle inside the pale blue smock as he pulled his fingers from the game slots. He nodded to the waiter, even though the tips were bloody.

"Lost again?" The waiter set the tall glass next to the many empty ones.

The medic closed one eye and peered up at the waiter, who was standing with his back to the sun.

"I made it to level fifteen once," the guy said, actually proud. His bluish-pink lips were thick and freckles peppered his pale skin.

"That's pure! I didn't know it went past level five! Did it actually hurt you?"

The waiter reached for the medic's hands but he'd wrapped them in a napkin then shoved them under the table next to his legs, which were – tiny! I stared amazed, at the shriveled limbs. Compared to the rest of his build, they were thin, awkward sticks.

That was when I noticed the wheelchair pushed in under the table. I couldn't believe it! I'd never seen one up close. A medic in a wheelchair? What was wrong with him? Purity had never let in anyone like him.

"It only hurt a bit." The medic shrugged and gazed blankly into his drink, as if he wanted the waiter to leave.

My stomach was twisting with hunger pains. Even the greasy smell coming from the café was agony.

The waiter eyed the game as he set the empty glasses on his tray, one at a time. "I could never get into Blass."

Why would you want to?

"It's not for everyone." The medic gripped his fingers inside the napkin. His orange-red hair hung over his eyes like a barrier. He turned from the waiter, who had finally loaded his tray.

I flagged him down.

"I'm starving. I've got to eat." Maybe I was rude but the waiter didn't seem to mind. I ordered a spiced soy-krill sandwich, a large tossed vamgula salad, watercress soup, and two glasses of water.

"Hope you're hungry." The waiter shook his head as he tapped my order into his wrist slate.

When he left, I rolled my head in slow circles, trying to ease the burning in my shoulder muscles, sore from carrying gear. The branches of a pine tree offered welcome shade, although I was still roasting. At least I didn't live farther south. The heatwaves there killed thousands every year.

With the ever-thinning ozone layer, the climate had been getting worse every year, even up north in Dawn. There had been freak rains, deadly dry spells, and snow in Africa once. When the energy freeze abruptly halted the glory days of careless consumption, fossil fuels became forbidden, and the scramble for new energy began. Now, it was harder to escape the increasing heat and the sun's blistering rays. I was surprised that Nature's Way Café could find the energy to cool its air, but I was sure it brought in more customers.

The metal fence around the patio was woven with real twigs and artificial leaves. Hardly natural. I stared out over the fence to the commons, where I'd just sketched that freakish woman. *Oh, Mur, why did this happen to me?*

Because you know how. Her voice was a gust of air through me.

Know how to what?

Draw into someone.

Is that what I did?

Yes.

Then someone in a gray-blue Academy uniform took a seat beside me.

"Jonah."

Even in a uniform, Jonah was delicious. I leaned toward him and inhaled his scent, finally feeling safe.

"I got your transmit." His voice rumbled, like the purr of a giant cat. "What's wrong?"

He wrapped an arm around me, kissing the top of my head between my two high braids.

"This disturbed woman," I began, "at the commons. She . . ."

"You missed class? I hope no one reports it."

"Forget about class, Jonah. Listen. The strangest thing happened."

"What?" Jonah twirled the tip of my braid through his fingers.

"I sketched a woman and . . . I can't describe it."

He lifted my chin to see my face, making me feel like a little kid who would be taken care of. His skin gleamed bronze, his teeth were startlingly white, and his eyes soothed me.

"Try," he said.

I pulled away, digging deep for the words. "Until now I've only sketched a reflection of people. Like in a mirror. But I drew this woman from the inside out. It was so pure!"

Jonah leaned closer, his eyes puzzled, searching. I was lucky I'd found him. He was the only one who tried to understand me. I reached into my bag, took out my slate, and showed him the sketch.

Jonah made a face. "Nice."

"I know. It's bizarre, but it's her. I mean, I love how I captured her, but that's not all. Afterward, I'd changed her. It's impossible, but the sunspots that had been on her hands and neck were gone."

"Gone? You're kidding."

"I'm not." I ignored my growling stomach, and the tight knot growing there. "But then she called me . . ." Dare I say it? ". . . skidge." I glanced quickly at Jonah for his reaction. "She said that Purity would get me."

"What would Purity want with you?" He rubbed my arm, an amused smile on his lips.

"I know." I sighed with relief. "But the sunspots?"

"You must have imagined them."

"How could I imagine that?"

"I don't know, but a portrait can't change a person."

"I didn't say the portrait changed her. I changed her. It's like I . . . healed her."

"You healed her?" Jonah laughed. "Do you know how hard it is to get rid of those sunspots?"

"I know." The idea was crazy. What was I saying?

"Remember when Jobey Mendleson got that improved sensory input package? His senses got so overloaded that he begged everyone to whisper and wouldn't eat anything spicier than bread until it wore off."

"What do you mean? You think I've had some kind of boost?"

Boosts were Purity's way of offering medical improvements without gen-eng, which permanently altered DNA. With boosts, you could get sensory enhancement, intelligence supplements, and other types, but they were either temporary or useless. Still, many people went for them, although I hadn't bothered.

"If you did, you didn't need to. You're already perfect."

I shook my head, but I had to smile. I knew he was distracting me with compliments, trying to ease my worries. Maybe he was right; maybe the sunspots had never been there. At least that's what I could tell Purity, if they came asking.

My stomach grumbled.

"Where's my sandwich? I'm going to faint if I don't eat soon." I glanced around for the waiter and caught the medic watching us. How much had he heard? Would he think I was skidge, too?

"A sandwich? That sure isn't a zero-residue food," Jonah teased.

The new zero-residue foods were all the rage with people who wanted to pretend they were just machines that didn't need to digest. No waste products. Just efficient food energy in a tasteless bar.

The medic looked away, still pouting. Maybe he hadn't been listening. I put on a smile for Jonah; I didn't want to make him endure any more of my worries. "I'm just an inefficient girl who is ravenously hungry for real food – waste and all."

Jonah wrinkled his nose in pretend disgust. Then he wound his arms around me and kissed my cheek. "That's what I like about you. You're a real traditional girl."

"Sure I am." I laughed and Jonah did too, showing the one tooth that stuck out slightly onto his lip. Jonah got annoyed when I pointed it out, so I resisted the temptation to touch it.

The waiter arrived with my food piled high and I untangled from Jonah. As Jonah ordered a drink, I noticed the medic sneaking looks at me. What had he heard? I worried again. Yet even with his eyes on me, I couldn't help but shovel great forkfuls of salad into my mouth and bite into the sandwich with gusto. The vinegary tang of the dressing and the salt of the sandwich made me thirsty. I gulped back half a glass of water.

Jonah told me his news while I ate. He had been chosen to work in the science labs at our school – the Academy of Intelligence. The Academy was Dawn's school for the unlucky few who'd shown superior talent. It was no reward – long school days with grueling assignments and weekend classes – yet Jonah never tired of it, and he couldn't wait to take on this new work. His experiments had to do with a spray-on second skin for protection against radiation. Maybe it would lead to a posting at the school. I listened, but the woman's words haunted me. *Are you skidge? Purity will be after you.*

Just as I was finishing the last of the sandwich, I noticed two officers in Purity uniforms searching the café. The same ones from the commons! I froze in mid-chew. That woman must have sent them to get me!

"Jonah!" I mumbled through my food. "Look!"

Jonah saw them and his eyes grew wide. I wanted to run and hide, but Jonah grabbed my hand and squeezed it.

"It's all right. They can't be here for you." Yet his eyes were worried.

I tried not to pull away. Purity held a brutal control over anyone with impure DNA, but those of us who were pure could still be questioned, held, and imprisoned for any supposed imperfections. It didn't take much.

I willed myself to be small enough to disappear. The Purity officers stopped to talk to the waiter at the inside counter. One officer was a tall, muscular man and the other was a smaller woman, her hair pulled back from her face and tucked under her hat. The man looked out through the window onto the patio at the guy with the Blass game. In seconds, he was beside him.

The officer nodded through the window at his partner, who was watching from inside the café. Then he said sternly, "Why did you run off?"

I let out a sigh. My muscles loosened. Of course they didn't want me. They wanted this guy. I should have known. Why would a medic be in a wheelchair? He must have escaped from a medical unit, or even Detention Block. Maybe he was dangerous. Maybe he'd snuck in from the Beyond and was infecting us right now. I'd been sitting alone with him, only two tables between us.

"Now, you know I can't run anywhere," the guy answered, awkwardly grabbing his game off the table with his hands still wrapped in the napkin. "I was just waiting here for you to pick me up."

How could he talk to a Purity officer that way? I waited for something terrible to happen, but the officer just seized the back of his wheelchair.

"Do you think he's skidge?" Jonah whispered, sneering at the game junky in his wheelchair. Jonah's top lip curled up in one corner, and for a moment he looked disagreeable, even unlikable.

I let go of Jonah's hand, which I'd been squeezing tightly. The guy must be some gen-eng experiment gone wrong. A good reason to be afraid of him. But the Purity officer had handled him in an easy way. No swarm and tackle; just a conversation. Maybe he wasn't dangerous.

"I don't know." I tried not to gape at them.

The waiter crept outside to watch. Others were peering through the café windows.

Then the woman officer came striding onto the patio, talking into a pocket slate in a rough, gravelly voice.

"Rylant here. We've got him. Repeat. We've got him." Her mouth was a hard line, her chin high, and her eyes as sharp as darts.

The male officer began to maneuver the wheelchair around the tables and tree trunks with expert precision.

The guy scowled. "I can steer myself."

He unwrapped his injured hands, which were still bleeding slightly. Then he flicked a switch on the arm of his wheelchair and rolled the steering ball under his palm

29

to direct the chair through the patio. The Purity officer retrieved the bloodied napkin, then followed him. I began to breathe easier. Then, just as they were about to leave, the guy in the wheelchair turned sideways and waved to us. What was he doing? I felt my cheeks redden.

The Purity officers paused to glance back suspiciously. *Don't breathe,* I thought. Rylant stabbed us with her eyes, as if she could see inside us. I couldn't look away. Were we next?

But she must have decided that we were no threat, because she nodded to her partner, then moments later, they were through the café and gone.

"Why did he do that?" Jonah's voice was loud and angry. "They might have thought we were with him. We could have been taken in for cleansing."

I released the air I'd been holding. Cleansing – I'd heard they rubbed you raw to remove any traces of impure DNA. My skin crawled. Yet for some strange reason, as I stared after that guy, I wished that I'd had the nerve to wave back.

mother

I woke to first light, still tired, the hint of a half-forgotten dream teasing me. I'd dreamed of letters, black on a white paper, that were too large to read. Like I was seeing them under a magnifying glass. Fuzzy edges of type. The fibers of the paper mashed together. Too close to read. Too close to understand. I'd tried to zoom out, to shift my head back, or to adjust a lever that would somehow bring the letters into focus. I'd called for Mur to help, but the message, if any, had remained blurred.

For days I'd dragged myself around – since I'd drawn that woman's portrait in the commons. I would fall asleep early, then wake before morning, sweating, dizzy, and hungry, but still exhausted. Only drawing set me free – gave me strength, energy. Running was the next best thing.

I made myself rise with the sun, forcing one foot in front of the other. Outside, the morning air smelled of rich earth, although the heat of the day would soon burn the sweetness into festering damp. I sprinted out into the forest, my bare feet thudding the dirt trail, jarring me with each step. The spiky evergreens were an emerald blur. The earth was firm under my feet. The trees swayed peacefully. If only I could outrun this pressure inside my chest. If only the wild forest could tame my fears.

Every day I'd waited for Purity to accuse me, to attack me with questions. That woman must have reported me. Was Purity watching? Would they confuse me with skidge? I felt eyes on me wherever I went.

I couldn't have healed that woman. It was impossible. Jonah had convinced me that I'd imagined her sunspots, but later, alone, I knew I had just let him persuade me. I'd seen it. The sunspots were there, and then they were gone. I was almost too scared to draw again.

I picked up my pace. The wind rushed over my body as if I were flying far from Dawn, from Purity, from everyone. If Purity were going to investigate me, they'd have to catch me first.

The run made me breathless, left my head still spinning. I sprinted out of the forest too fast and back onto the streets of Dawn. Back to cruel reality. My heart pounded faster. The trim grass parallel to the street was wet with dew. I slowed my pace. My shoes would have had a better grip, but bare feet on the earth helped me feel solid.

As I jogged past boring, identical housing units, an ache in my side forced me to slow even more. My mouth tasted sour and my breath came in gasps. I was weaker than a slug.

I stopped running as I neared my own unit with its bushes forced into annoying, neat shapes by Mother. Birds chirped and twittered across the street in the forest. Soon the heat of the day would silence them. Pacing around on the small patch of grass, I willed my heart to slow and my legs to stop trembling. If only running could end this weakness – and the feeling that Purity might come for me at any moment.

Come on, I thought. *You know you're pure.*

My last medical scan – could it have had some strange affect on me? Had I become skidge without knowing it? No, that was impossible.

Yet an image stuck in my mind, like a nagging voice: the woman's healed hands and neck. How could I explain them?

I bent at the waist and stretched the back of my legs. Painful but good. I held the stretch and tried to breathe evenly.

The grass was sparse by the pines near me where the fallen needles had destroyed almost all life. But poking through the brown layer of needles were green sprigs of lifewort. Determined things.

At least I'd discovered a new sketching technique. Drawing intuitively, with my eyes closed. Exciting. Intriguing. Mur had something to do with that, and I did want to try it again, as long as nothing strange happened.

I finished stretching and headed in, my rubbery legs protesting every movement.

It was no cooler inside. As I shut the door, I could hear the announcer for the *New North Report*. From the hall I saw Dad in the front room, short and squat on the couch, a slate in hand. He was watching the large display screen while reading and making notes, the sunlight reflecting off the rounded sheen of his head.

"Hey, Dad."

He glanced at me. Crumbs littered the table in front of him. "Lenni, did you get your assignment done on the colonization of Mars? And what about your robotics work? How's that coming?"

"Fine. Everything's fine." He didn't ask about me, just my Academy work.

"Keeping up, are you? Good. You know, I used to run for ninety minutes before dawn."

"So you've told me." *Not that anyone could tell, from your paunch.*

"Sorry, I guess you knew that." He regarded me with a quizzical look. "Did you change something? You look different somehow . . . ."

"Not much new." *Just sucked dry, drained, and left in the sun too long. Nothing to worry about,* I wanted to say. *Oh, yeah, Dad, and Purity's about to take me in.*

Then the screen changed and distracted him.

"I have always argued that genetic engineering denies the natural order of things," said a male voice from the *New North Report*. "Someday we'll deeply regret it. Because the more we select for a particular trait, the more we counter-select other traits. And we can't measure this relationship. This is the case with lifeweed."

Dad snorted. "Lifewort," he corrected.

I wiped my feet, leaving brown smears on the mat to infuriate Mother. A petty satisfaction, but well worth it.

"Lifeweed was created by Dawn's own GrowTech to survive its enemies by using natural mechanisms," continued the voice.

GrowTech. The reporter was talking about Dad's company. I eased into the room so I could see the screen better. A stern man with graying hair was talking. Dad was frowning.

"But what it means for humans is that it's impossible to kill. It's taking over our natural spaces and choking our farms. How can we rid ourselves of this invasive, unwelcome plant?"

"You have no vision, Hubert." Dad narrowed his eyes at the screen.

"You know him?" I plopped onto the couch.

"Sure, he's my nemesis, and a voice for Purity." He squeezed my hand to tell me to be quiet.

A woman appeared in a field overrun with lifewort. "Lifeweed, originally called lifewort by the company that created it, can be processed into an oil used to make biodegradable plastics. However, it was nicknamed lifeweed by its detractors once it was proven to be invasive. This seemingly useful plant is now damaging crops, parks, and entire ecosystems."

"Is that true?" I thought of the patch under the pines, where nothing else would grow. I wouldn't want lifewort to take over, but I admired it.

"Lies. All lies. Hubert is behind it."

Hubert flashed onto the screen again. "We prohibit any gen-eng of humans that would permanently alter the gene pool. So how can we allow a company to modify plant or animal DNA? It's an act of controlling the future, obliterating life as we know it. Like humans, DNA modifications of plants and animals should be limited to repair, rather than subject to permanent enhancement. GrowTech should be forced to cease all research in this area and provide the funds to clean up this mess."

"What's the difference between carefully bred plants and genetic engineering?" Dad snorted again. "You notice they didn't ask my opinion."

"If we don't watch out," Hubert continued, "GrowTech will begin experimenting on humans next. Then we'll be no better off than the Beyond. Isn't that why we support our Purity communities – to escape the chaos of two-headed babies and designer viruses? We can't pass the negative effects of our experimentation onto future generations. We have to stay pure."

"Oh, please." Dad wiped a hand over his face.

This guy is a fanatic, I thought, *and he's after Dad.* I glanced at my father, wondering how he put up with this.

A news anchor appeared behind a circular desk. "In other news, the latest massive solar grid, which was expected to be operational by December, was sabotaged last night. No group has come forward to claim responsibility, and officials expect the new power allowances to be delayed until next summer."

I groaned. "Not another power shortage!" I had only a little time for sketching as it was.

"As if Hubert isn't enough," Dad's voice was gruff, "now Dawn will have to justify its power requirements."

Then Dad must have caught the pained look on my face because he said, "Dawn will purchase more power allowances. We'll get through it, somehow."

Dad had often told me why he and Mother had applied to come to Dawn, long before I was born. Violent climate changes had made the cooler temperatures of the north attractive. Mother had wanted a pure community without bizarre, half-human genetic creations running about. And the Purity settlements had promised support for GrowTech as well as a stable energy supply. If only that were true.

He squeezed my hand again, this time as a comfort.

I squeezed back. Dad was a maniac workaholic who wanted me to match his frantic schedule, but he cared.

A Purity ad had begun babbling on the display screen. "The Genetic Purity Council protects you and your family from the horrors of this world every day." A picture appeared of a malformed beast attacking a young boy, reminding me of that creepy transgenic in the commons that had gone for my toes. "Help Purity grow by donating generously to the settlement expansion campaign." The screen showed happy settlers building new housing units. "Together we'll forge the future with a pure human race. Purity – Committed to Tomorrow."

"Screen off." Dad stood abruptly, knocking his slate onto the rug. The screen went blank. "I've got to go." Dad grunted as he leaned over to pick up his slate. When he had straightened, his face was red and puffy. "You can imagine the day I have ahead of me. I'm sure Purity will be investigating GrowTech, yet again." He shuffled out of the room. "Take care of yourself," he said from the hall. "You're looking tired today."

If only that were it. With a knot of worry in my stomach, I walked down the long hall to the kitchen. Power shortages and Purity propaganda – I could do without either. And I couldn't shake the feeling that Purity, or someone else, was watching me.

From the front of our unit, Dad called, "Lenni? Your mother wants to see you this morning. Be sure you talk to her." The front door slammed.

Of course she did. She was unavoidable.

The footsteps of Mother and Elyle echoed from the stairs. Mother insisted on scrutinizing me each morning, and was always waiting for me after the Academy. If I dodged her, she'd trail me to school. I couldn't begin to understand why. I just tried to endure it.

In the kitchen, I prepared two sliced apples sprinkled with cinnamon, toast with Nutrio spread, and orange juice. I eyed the energy consumption gauge beside the sink, watching the numbers slowly blink higher and higher. *As if we'd ever have enough.* I carried my tray into the sunroom.

The room was full of rich green leaves, the fragrance of flowers, and the undercurrent of rot. Mother and Elyle were there – Mother in oversized glasses that magnified her eyes. Of course, she didn't need glasses. Anyone could get lens implants, but doctors made her nervous – ever since they'd hauled her to a medical unit during a prolonged crisis. She'd howled and tried to get back home, but they'd called it a breakdown and kept her longer. It'd been the easiest six months of my life, except for the visits.

I sat at the table and took a large crunchy bite of toast.

"Morning." Elyle nodded a friendly hello.

I tried to smile back with my mouth full. "Morning," I mumbled through my food.

Elyle padded across the room to shut a window from the heat of the day. She moved with the grace of a cat, even though she was a few years older than Mother. The smell of lavender always clung to her.

"You're a delicate girl, Lenni. Please, eat like one." Mother was using tiny shears to prune her plants.

The tangy spread turned sour in my mouth. How could she make anything grow?

"Can't you even say good morning before you tell me what to do?" I took another bite.

"I'm only trying to help," Mother said, using her lecturing voice. "You're capable of so much. You need to do your best, always."

"I'm just eating toast!"

Mother's hand, holding the shears, began to shake. Great. Now, I'd done it.

Elyle studied the two of us. She came to stand behind my chair and smoothed my hair. I looked up at her. Her eyes flickered like tiger's-eye gems – brown at the edges moving into a shining gold. Let it go, her expression said.

I tried to calm down. Breathe. Be like Elyle. Nothing Mother did could upset her.

"Mara," Elyle spoke to Mother, her tone gentle, "should I fix you an elixir?"

When I was a baby, Elyle was hired as my nurse-maid, but now she cared more for Mother than for me. Elyle was her shadow. Always there, always nurturing. How could Elyle stand her?

"Oh, Elyle, you're so good to me." Mother sat heavily in a chair, dropped the shears into her lap, then put a fat hand to her forehead. "Lemon and licorice, please."

Elyle headed for the kitchen. I made myself swallow my anger along with my food. I tried not to glare at the bucket of daffodils that Mother had forced to flower out of season. Mother fanned herself with her hand and breathed in rapid bursts. The air was tight between us.

Minutes later, Elyle returned with the elixir, and Mother drank in slow, full gulps.

"Elyle, I owe you my life, as always."

"I would accept no such gift." Elyle smiled.

I bit into a cinnamon apple, but the intense smell of the elixir overpowered its sweetness. My nose twitched. I watched Mother power back the elixir.

"Now, Lenni, we have something to discuss," Mother began when she'd recovered. "The Academy has informed me that you did not attend classes on Saturday."

I hardened into stone, my hand clasped in a fist around my napkin. I needed an explanation, fast.

"Don't try to give me any excuses."

How did she know what I was thinking?

"Perhaps you need Elyle to help you find your way to the Academy?"

I cringed, although I was surprised she wouldn't want to do it herself.

"Now, do you want to tell me where you were instead of school?"

"Well, uh . . ."

"We're trying to do our best for you." For a moment, Mother's eyes saddened, her eyebrows knotted. "After your disappointing performance last year . . ."

"My assessment was excellent!" I looked at Elyle, expecting her to help.

"Now, Mara . . ." Elyle began.

". . . and your strange preoccupation with art . . ." Mother pronounced *art* with a hard, sharp *T*. "I can't trust you to know what's good for you."

Why did I get *her* for a mother? I couldn't wait for Elyle to smooth this over.

I stood, pushing my chair back so hard that it toppled over with a satisfying crash. "If I did tell you where I was, would you even try to understand?" I yelled, facing Mother down, with only the gray of the table between us. "No. You want to control my life. No friends. No fun. Nothing but the Academy."

"It's for your own good, Lenni," Mother's voice cracked. "If only you knew the sacrifices I've made for you. If only you . . ."

"That's enough, Mara." Elyle's voice held a warning.

Mother stopped, stunned. As if she'd said too much.

"You're not the only one who's made sacrifices!" I shouted.

Elyle shushed me. Her back to Mother, she mouthed, "Keep her calm."

Keep Mother calm, the doctor had said, but who cared about me? Still, I bit my tongue, remembering her last episode. It could get worse.

"You seem a bit pale, Mara," Elyle continued. "Do you need to lie down?"

"What?" Mother mumbled. "Yes, I am lightheaded today."

"Let me help you to your room." Elyle helped Mother up and guided her around the table, then sagged as she began to support most of Mother's weight.

I threw my napkin on the table and stomped past them, feeling invaded, controlled. I was missing some vital ingredient that would satisfy Mother – get her off my back. Never enough. Never pleased. No matter what I did, it was wrong. So why bother? I would do what I wanted, when I wanted. She could order me around, but she wasn't in charge.

waterstone

"Lenni?"

I was sketching in the front room. I quickly switched off my slate, jammed it into my shoulder bag, and hurried to the door to get into the gray shoes I had to wear to the Academy. The smell of sunblock on my legs reminded me of sunshine and sweat, the lakeside commons and drawing – and Purity.

Elyle came down the stairs and into the hall. "Oh, it's you," I said, tying my shoes. Not Mother. Good. She would have started a lecture about sketching.

I was wearing the blue-gray shirt and knee-length shorts of the Academy uniform, although I hated looking the same as everyone else. It made me feel like I was a clone.

"I have something to show you," Elyle said.

Elyle had found a moment away from Mother. "What is it?" I asked, curious.

Elyle's cheeks rounded with her smile, and gentle layers of wrinkles deepened around her eyes. "You have time before school. Come."

She padded off down the hall. I followed, intrigued. Mother demanded most of Elyle's attention, but when Elyle sought me out it was always worth it. Like when we'd hiked to the waterfall and swum in the lake. The water had been cool and the sky wide open.

In the basement, the tile floor echoed our footsteps. I squinted at the bright artificial lights. We were heading toward Elyle's workroom, a place she kept strictly private. I sucked in a breath. *Please, Elyle, show me inside.*

Once, when I was about six, I tried to sneak into Elyle's workroom. I'd had the door open a crack when Elyle's hand gripped my shoulder. "Not for you." She had brought me upstairs and given me creamy fudge and a firm lecture. The taste of fudge still made me feel guilty. I hadn't gone near her workroom since. Even Mother didn't go in.

Elyle stopped in front of the wooden door to her workroom. I didn't dare speak, but I desperately wanted to know what she kept in there. When Elyle slid open the door, I peered over her shoulder, eager to get a look.

Muted colors, a floral scent. Elyle snapped on the single overhead bulb. The room was smaller than I had expected and it was decorated with exotic stone sculptures and silk wall hangings. Shelves on one wall held several small, rough stones and a large lump shrouded in white cloth. Elyle was an artist, too!

I followed her in. She should have told me. We could have shared so much. Yet, I knew why Elyle had kept her secret. In Dawn, art could be dangerous if Purity didn't like it. And Mother would never approve. At least Elyle was sharing now. I felt honored, trusted.

"Here." Elyle motioned toward a basin with a plastic tube hanging over it like a faucet. Water streamed from the tube onto a medallion-shaped object that was suspended by a wire mechanism. "Your waterstone."

"My waterstone?"

I heard a soft whir. A pump in a large tank on the floor sent water flowing steadily through the tube and over the object.

Elyle nodded. "Finally finished."

Her eyes misted over. She turned a tap and the water slowed, then stopped. I leaned over her shoulder as she loosened the wires and removed the stone.

Why had she made it for me? What did it mean? I was bursting with questions, but I knew Elyle well enough to hold them back. Her explanations were never rushed, and she revealed herself with the same agonizing pace as clouds meandering across the sky.

She ran her hand over the stone, caressing its edges and curves, then held it up for me to see. The speckled gray and green stone was about the size of an egg, only flat and round. The water had shaped the stone so that a raised image had emerged in the center, its textures and colors suggesting the fluid figure of a woman bending to reach something distant, untouchable.

I stroked the stone. It was wet and cold, but my hand warmed it, brought it life. I pulled back.

45

"Why?" I couldn't hold in my questions any longer.

Elyle smiled at me. "I've been shaping this since I came – just after you were born. My husband conceived the craft, but I altered his basin and tube."

"You're married?" I'd never heard of a husband, never heard much about Elyle at all. She'd always evaded my questions.

"I was." Elyle looked away, but not before I caught her sad expression.

"What happened?" I couldn't help prying. Elyle married – it was so intriguing.

"He passed away suddenly. It was a hiking accident." She turned back, her eyes brighter than usual. "He called his technique 'spirit shaping,'" she said, clearly halting further discussion of her past. "He used water to discover a person's soul."

Like my portrait of that woman, I thought. Maybe Elyle would understand.

"The stone is a protection, too. An amulet to guard the soul against those who seek to harm it." She paused. "I've made a few in my time. Have one myself that my husband made for me. I made your mother one, too. Don't show them around, though. Private stuff."

Mother tolerated a waterstone, but sketching was a frivolous waste of time? Now, that was fair. A hot flush of anger flared up inside, but I forced it back down, not willing to ruin this moment with Elyle.

"Can I hold it?" I studied the stone, looking for its hidden truths. It was so much like that portrait – capturing the essence of that woman. I'd seen inside her, understood her.

"It's yours now." Elyle smiled again, then placed my waterstone reverently in my hand. "You're ready to understand it."

"Oh, thank you, Elyle," I cradled the stone. "But what do you mean – I'm ready to understand it?"

"Just what I said. Learn from it. Keep it with you always."

She seemed to think that this stone could answer all my questions. I studied it again, skeptically this time.

Elyle began adjusting a new stone in the wire mechanism. She moved the thin tube so that it hung over the stone and turned the tap back on.

I breathed in the water's fragrance. "Lavender?" Elyle's familiar smell.

"It's actually a blend of oils designed to awaken the form within the stone."

She slowed the water's flow a little. Only the trickle of liquid and the whir of the pump broke the silence.

Then the pump stalled and sputtered. Elyle leaned down and tapped it with her fingers.

"Don't quit on me now."

The pump sputtered back to life.

Elyle watched the pump critically, and I watched her, wondering at this new side to her. I'd lived with Elyle for over fifteen years and often felt more connected to her than my own parents. Now, I understood why. Elyle was an artist, like I was. Tears found my eyes.

Then Elyle said, "Your mother, she has her good side. You see how she nurtures those plants? How she helps them bloom?"

My body tensed at the mention of Mother. I nodded slowly.

"She's worried about you, trying to care for you."

"Maybe I don't want to bloom when she demands it."

"She needs help. And so do you, more than you know." Elyle headed for the door. "That's why I'm here. That's why I made you a waterstone."

"Oh, Elyle. Why do you stay with us?" I wiped my eyes, thinking of the years Elyle had spent with us, sacrificed for us, to help Mother and me. She made home bearable, but why did she bother?

"Lenni, I could never leave. You and Mara and Leonard have become my family, and I'd do anything to protect you."

"You would?" I followed her into the brilliant white hall, liking the idea that Elyle was family. Many times, as a kid, I'd wished she were my mother, or at least related to me in some way. I guess after all these years she was family, although I still couldn't figure out why she'd want to be.

"I would. So let me help." She slid her workroom door shut.

"I'll try." My voice echoed with an empty ring.

jonah's portrait

For a whole week, I'd done what everyone expected of me: gone to class, completed the work, and kept from sketching, in case another strange event happened. Now, I was on a shaded bench at the lakeside commons, running my fingers over the smooth curves of my waterstone, and missing Academy classes again.

I just have to figure some things out, then I'll go to class, I thought. But the sky was so blue and the lake was such a swirling green of reflected trees that I couldn't make myself leave. Mur had sent me to the commons to sketch for some reason, maybe to discover that new technique. She must have had some grand design, some reason I couldn't see.

Part of me hoped that the woman I'd sketched would descend upon me, without Purity, so I could understand what had really happened that day. But it was Jonah who appeared, blocking my view, in an Academy uniform that matched my own.

I flushed and smoothed some damp hair off my face, wanting to look nice for him and hating myself for trying too hard. "What are you doing here?"

Jonah sat on the bench. "I could ask you the same thing."

I shoved my waterstone into my pocket. My bag was scrunched between us and my slate was on my lap. Only a few people were hurrying through the courtyard – the heat was too oppressive to linger. No one to spy on us. Mother could never know about Jonah.

"I'm sketching."

Although I wasn't really. I was only thinking about sketching, about how my life was dull without it. All that was left were my parents – who planned my days for me – and the droning classes at the Academy.

Jonah glanced at my blank slate then pierced me with his eyes, as if he could pierce a hole into my soul and expose me.

"Maybe you should sketch me. I'm ready for a portrait."

"What?" I stared at him. I'd sketched Jonah before, but not in my new way. "But what if I . . .?" I stopped.

So what if I sketched him, connected with him, even healed him, not that he needed it. Sketching Jonah was no chore.

"I'll do it." I sat up straight and cleared the screen on my slate. Jonah knew just how to help.

"Good." He adjusted himself on the bench, one arm dangling casually over the back and his feet planted solidly on the ground. "What do I do?"

"Nothing. I don't know. Just sit. I have to find you."

I got my slate and stylus ready, then gazed steadily at him. Nerve-wracking, meeting his eyes like that without talking. It had been easier with a stranger. Yet when I had him solid in my mind, I shut my eyes and began to trace his image over again on the back of my eyelids.

Help me, Mur.

Then Mur was with me, a trusted friend.

I will.

Her voice was the rush of a cool spring breeze, and I followed the playful flow of her. Gradually, I could sense my artist fingers reaching out for the energy that was Jonah. My skin grew hot and my blood pumped faster. Amazed and relieved that I could do it again, I extended my energy into his.

His wide mouth was level with mine. His face, his whole body, glowed like a bronzed statue. His radiance pulled me toward him with a magnetic force. Our legs and arms meshed; our bodies fused like two beings sharing the same heart.

Don't let it end, I thought, like some corny, love-struck fool.

Never, I heard Jonah say.

My eyes burst open in surprise. Instantly I shut them again, wanting to get back to Jonah. He could hear me. He had answered me. It had been so pure. I had to get close to him again. But I was too late. The connection was broken. I ached, wanting it back.

"No," I moaned.

My heart was still beating fast and my head pounded.

I opened my eyes again, searching Jonah's face. His eyes were wide, his lips parted.

"Did you hear . . ." I began.

"Yes," he answered, without letting me finish. "I don't know how you did it, but . . . wow!" He grinned and squeezed my hand.

Then, as if we were still connected, we both glanced down at the portrait together.

The slate showed the swirl of two figures dancing, with legs, arms, torsos entwined. Jonah's body was stretched tall and filled with such energy that he might move off the screen. Like a bad omen, my own image was fractured by hairline cracks, giving me the appearance of a glass figurine about to shatter.

I let the slate fall into my lap and looked back at Jonah, pushing my image from my mind. My hands were hot and trembling. I breathed deeply to still the pulsing energy in my head. Jonah pressed closer and kissed me, his velvet lips sliding over mine. So pure! I knew I belonged with Jonah. My whole body screamed for him. I couldn't stand to be separated. We'd started a raging fire and I wasn't going to extinguish it.

"Get away from her!"

Mother? It was her voice! I saw Jonah's surprised eyes, gaping at something behind me.

Please, no. Don't let it be her.

I spun, clenching my teeth, bracing for the attack. Mother. She was wearing an electric blue dress of special fibers to block the sun's rays. Light glinted off her huge studded sunglasses, and she was holding a solar fan in her chubby pink hand. She looked eccentric, bizarre – toxic. What would Jonah think?

"You should leave now," Mother told Jonah, her voice shrill.

"No, you don't have to go." How dare she order him around!

Jonah didn't move. He glanced from Mother to me, confused.

Mother stepped into the shade, removed her sunglasses, and scrutinized Jonah. "Well, a polite young man wouldn't make me stand in this heat!" Her eyelids fluttered weakly.

"Stop it!" She just wanted to chase him away. I tasted blood, then realized I was biting my lip. My head still ached but I ignored it. I had to pay attention. I had to handle Mother.

Jonah vaulted off the bench. He stepped backward until he bumped into some low shrubs, then fell. He was back on his feet in seconds.

"You can't trust anyone, Lenni." Mother wilted onto the bench, dropping her sunglasses, beads of sweat decorating her forehead. "You let people get too close. I try to protect you, but . . . oh, this heat makes me faint."

She was talking crazy. I tried to swallow the lump in my throat. No yelling. Deal with her. Only a few months ago, Mother had collapsed during an argument with Dad. I had to keep her calm.

With as much sweetness as possible, I said, "Jonah, meet my mother." I hated to admit this creature was related to me. Yet if I could smooth this over, quiet Mother down, maybe I could make this work out.

Jonah stepped forward, looking relieved to have something to do, and put out his hand. I hoped he noticed there was no family resemblance. "Glad to meet you."

Thanks, Jonah, I thought. He was behaving better than Mother.

Mother refused his hand. "I'm sorry, Jonah, but Lenni has a policy of no male friends. Her studies keep her much too busy."

"Oh." Jonah pulled back his hand and looked at me for help.

"Mother!" I stood. I wanted to strike her.

"Lenni, do you know what I've been through?" Her voice wobbled. "First the Academy tells me you missed your classes *again,* then I find you with this . . . this . . . *boy?*" She fluttered a hand at Jonah, who was staring, open-mouthed. "I have to watch your every move!"

"You were following me? Spying? How dare you!" Tension traveled up my spine, making my muscles tight. "You had no right . . . ." My voice rose to a shriek.

"How can I keep you safe when you won't listen?" She let out a low moan. "Oh, even in the shade I'm done for." Her eyes had that familiar glazed look.

"No, Mother. Don't!" I yelled.

Mother shriveled and faded in an instant. Her skin paled, and her eyes rolled back in her head until only the whites showed. Her fan fell to the ground and stopped buzzing.

"Is she all right?" Jonah sounded alarmed.

Mother lay slumped across the bench. I glanced around desperately for Elyle. She had to be nearby. If Mother was here, so was she.

"I . . . I don't know."

It was my fault. I shouldn't have challenged her. But she was so infuriating. I had to defend myself. I felt her pulse. Steady.

"Mother?" I shook her gently.

She didn't budge. Her eyes weren't moving under the lids. I shook her again. Her head slumped lower.

"What can we do? What's wrong with her?"

"I . . . uh . . ." I could say that my mother was paranoid, overprotective, and manipulative. It was true, but even Jonah might not understand. "She's ill, sometimes."

Jonah didn't answer.

Then, Elyle appeared, breathless from running across the grass. She raised one eyebrow at Jonah, then broke a capsule in half and held it under Mother's nose.

"Can I help?" Jonah asked.

Ignoring him, Elyle caressed Mother's cheeks and whispered into her ear.

Mother's eyes fluttered open. She groaned.

I tried not to cry. What did Jonah think of me now? I'd made Mother collapse. What did he think of my mother? I wished she were normal. *Oh, Mur, I wish you could fix all this.*

"I need your help, Lenni," Elyle called, trying to lift Mother off the bench.

I helped Mother to the car, numb with guilt and embarrassment. Jonah followed with my bag. If only I could have disappeared with him. If only Mother didn't poison everything.

I didn't cry until I heard the buzz of the car's electric engine. We pulled away from the commons, away from Jonah, and tears streamed down my cheeks, staining my uniform dark blue. I could have cracked into pieces. I was being pulled apart by conflicting forces. Splintering, just like my image in Jonah's portrait.

letters

I flopped onto my bed and embraced my pillow. I couldn't stop seeing Jonah silently watching me leave. I'd left him behind, just like Mother had planned. I punched my pillow, wanting to scream.

Mother would control my every move. I'd never get time with Jonah now, even if he did want to see me again. I'd probably lost him forever.

The room blurred as tears pooled in my eyes and began to trickle down my cheeks. My bag was still looped around my shoulder. I tugged it off, and flung it to the floor.

At least Mother hadn't seen the sketch of Jonah. Although Elyle had glanced at my slate. She'd tried to talk to me about it in the car, but I'd refused. That sketch was private. And hadn't she known about Mother's spying? She should have warned me. She'd promised to protect me. No wonder I'd felt watched. It hadn't been Purity spying on me; it was a more personal betrayal.

I licked a stray tear and tasted warm salt.

Oh, Jonah. I miss you already.

Sketching would help me feel better. Wiping my cheeks dry with one arm, I wormed to the edge of the bed and stretched down to retrieve my slate from my bag. As I powered it up, my hand itched to draw, yet when I thought again of Jonah's portrait, I changed my mind. I couldn't sketch on my slate just yet. I couldn't be reminded of what had happened with Mother. And, there was my power allowance. I was probably close to my weekly limit. I rummaged around in my bag until I found some homemade paper and a pencil.

With my hand clutched tight around the pencil, I stared down at the rough paper. Strange how I was in his sketch – how the two of us had been caught in that dance. Jonah gave me reason to breathe. I couldn't be separated from him.

I flipped the paper onto my bed, unable even to try to draw. Incredible – how we'd connected. How I'd known him in a wonderful new way. Now I'd never see him. Mother would be sure to make that impossible. A sharp shard of pain cut through me.

Enough. I marched over to my full-length mirror with paper and pencil in hand. I pulled a chair up to the mirror, sat down, and studied myself.

I shut my eyes and began to draw. My pencil bumped and jerked over the surface. Ultra-smooth sheets made from lifewort plastic had replaced traditional paper, but there was something about my rough homemade paper that I preferred.

Drawing without a slate was awkward. I stopped to check my sketch. A close-up – a poor likeness of the nose, cheeks, and eyes I saw in the mirror.

No, I thought. *It's all wrong.*

I flipped the sheet over, glanced at my image in the mirror, shut my eyes, and began again. The curves of my chin, neck, and shoulders.

No. No.

I took up another sheet. The bumpy texture of the paper was a familiar brush against the side of my hand now. This time I drew my hand with fingers tight around a pencil, then long legs with one foot pointed, then the bend of my elbow.

Again and again, I drew pieces of myself until the carpet was scattered with half-finished sketches. Puzzle pieces that somehow formed a whole.

I'm just wasting paper, I thought. I could draw into others, connect to Jonah, but I couldn't do this.

Stop it. Breathe. I pulled my waterstone from my pocket, where I'd kept it faithfully since Elyle had given it to me. Could it give me answers? The figure on the stone was reaching out. Her gesture was flowing and graceful, not stiff and scattered. *Imitate her,* I thought. Rubbing the stone, I stared at the papers on the floor and at myself in the mirror until I calmed. Then I shut my eyes again.

I concentrated on Mur. *Guide me, Mur. I need to draw.*

This way, she replied, tugging me inward.

My eyes rolled backward as if I could look inside at myself. Then I began to dot the page with the pencil. Flecks and tiny lines weaving together. Dense here, loose

there. I let my hand reveal the picture. Something familiar. Something I knew. What was it? I pushed the question
away, afraid to stop the movement of my hand.

When my hand slowed, I opened my eyes.
Gradually, I recognized the arrangement of dots and lines.
My dream — the one I couldn't decipher. Tiny dots that
were so close together they formed shapes, patterns.
Letters — black on a white paper — that were magnified.
Too large to read. I let the idea move through me until I
could see what the letters were spelling.

My own name: Lenni. Made from a pattern of
dots. Like cells that fuse together somehow to create a
whole person. Parts of a whole.

In my dream, I'd been desperate to see more than
just dots. Now, I could finally see the whole shape — my
name — but it was fractured again, just like in my sketch
with Jonah. Another bad omen. I hugged my knees,
wondering what it all meant.

the academy

"She doesn't own me. She can't make me walk with you." I burst out the door into the morning heat. Walked to school by Elyle. It was beyond embarrassing.

I leapt ahead, through Mother's garden. Mother had clipped the yew and forced a butterfly bush to flower in spite of the heat, but at least new sprigs of lifewort were keeping pace.

Elyle matched my steps. "Well, you did miss school twice. And you broke her rules with that boy."

Jonah. I hadn't dared to transmit to him last night. How could I explain? Today, at the Academy, I would talk to him. Mother couldn't stop me from seeing him there.

"She was spying on me." I raised my voice. "Why didn't you tell me about that?"

"She wasn't spying. The Academy transmitted that you weren't in class and we went looking for you. We were worried."

"You said you would help." I walked faster.

"Slow down, Lenni. I'm not the enemy. Neither is your mother."

I sighed, then slowed. "I know." Mother was ill; it was hard to remember that when she was so controlling.

We walked along the side of the road in silence. When we reached the corner where the street widened, other people appeared, walking, on bikes, or in solar-electric cars. Everyone would see me walking with Elyle. I put my head down to avoid their eyes.

"Do you want to talk about your sketches?" Elyle said.

"What?" I frowned. This wasn't a friendly stroll; it was a punishment.

"Your sketches. How are they going?"

I stared at the scuffed toes of my Academy shoes. Elyle had made me a waterstone. She would understand, but this was too personal to discuss on the street, surrounded by people.

Trust her, came Mur's voice.

And I knew Mur was right. How often did I get Elyle to myself?

The words slipped out without effort. In a low voice, I told Elyle about my new portraits, and the healing. I told her how good sketching felt. How everything else faded away until I was the stylus and Mur was drawing with me.

"You still hear Mur?" Elyle raised one eyebrow.

"Yes." Mur was almost too private to share. Only once before, when I was seven, had I ever mentioned her.

"Did you hear what Mur said?" I'd asked Elyle. We'd been drinking juice at the table. Mother was asleep in a huge pillowed chair. Even then she was ill.

"Mur?"

"Yes, Mur. She tells me things. There, see her silver hair?" I'd pointed to where she stood among Mother's plants.

"Hush," Elyle had said in her calm, caring voice. She lowered my finger, glancing at Mother. "Most hear only themselves."

"You don't hear her?" I'd been confused. How could that be?

"No." Her eyes had shown she was far away, dreaming, or maybe wishing. "I muddle through on my own."

I'd been sad then. Sad for those who were only one.

We were stopped under a row of locust trees now, halfway to the Academy. Sunlight filtered through the leaves onto Elyle's face.

"Look at my portraits." I offered her my slate.

Elyle took it and gazed intently at each sketch, one by one. People rushed around us on both sides. Not one person bothered to look at my slate. I had nothing to worry about. No one else cared about my sketches.

"Lenni," Elyle began when she saw the woman's portrait from the commons. "It's like you sketched her soul." Tears collected in her eyes.

I nodded, staring at Elyle, wanting to hug her, to cry out, to celebrate. She understood. She really understood. The scent of lavender enveloped me.

Elyle wiped her eyes. Her face grew serious.

"When you first told me about Mur, I knew you were . . ." Elyle paused, ". . . special. But some people might think Mur is imaginary – that you're hearing things. Keep her to yourself, all right?"

"Don't worry about that. I'd never tell anyone." I glanced around, but no one was bothering to eavesdrop. A crowd was the best place to hide.

We walked side by side. Our footsteps found a matching rhythm. A fresh breeze pushed us from behind. All the faces in the crowd were portraits to be drawn, souls to be sketched. I swung my arms, suddenly calmer. Elyle made me feel that I could last a little longer with Mother, with the Academy, with everything.

When we reached the edge of Center Block, Elyle said good-bye, sparing me the humiliation of delivering me to the Academy's doorstep. I wove through the crowd, searching for Jonah. Center Block was filled with uniforms scurrying toward the towering buildings that lined the square like soldiers on parade. The sports complex, medical unit, Academy of Intelligence, offices of GrowTech, and Purity headquarters – all trying to outdo each other. Yet Purity had the tallest tower, with a huge billboard flashing, COMMITTED TO TOMORROW.

I kept an eye out for Purity officers as I dodged around a group of fanatics gathered with signs that read, KEEP BACK THE BEYOND. Militants for Purity. We were supposed to meet in the square for "like-minded discussions" and "matters of interest to the settlement," but any gatherings were just praise for Purity. I followed the other gray-blue uniforms to the Academy, still looking for Jonah.

The Academy was a four-storey building wedged in beside the main medical unit. The Purity headquarters across the square made me uncomfortable. I thought I saw the stern-faced officer from the café – Rylant had been her name – going into the medical unit.

I hurried up the stone stairs, through the double glass doors, and into the main hall of the Academy. The air was no cooler, the noise echoed off the high ceiling, and there was no sign of Jonah.

I checked the bench under the huge spiral staircase to the second floor, our usual meeting spot. No Jonah. Maybe he was avoiding me. Maybe he didn't want to talk or even be with me. I thought of the connection with him and ached for it.

Back by the doors, I scanned the hall again. Five minutes until first lecture. *Come on, Jonah.*

Then I caught sight of the game junky from the café in an Academy uniform. What was he doing here?

He was in his wheelchair, glaring at the tall staircase. His hair had been shaved to a bright-orange stubble all over his head. *I should show him the lift,* I thought, but I didn't move.

He glanced over the crowd, stopping on me, a glint of recognition in his eyes. I started. He remembered me. I hoped he didn't remember my conversation with Jonah. I spun around, panicked that he might tell someone what he'd heard, and whacked into a familiar chest.

"Jonah!"

He smiled. A good sign. "Hey, Lenni."

"Oh, Jonah, I'm so sorry about yesterday." People jostled and bumped us, but I didn't care.

"Sorry for what?"

"For Mother."

Jonah grinned. "Your mother? Don't worry. I have one, too." He kissed me on the nose, then glanced around quickly to check that no professors had noticed. "What do I have to do to get another portrait like that? What you did – that was incredible!"

A laugh burbled from deep inside. "I'll sketch you now."

I wanted to hold him again, to sketch him over and over. Mother couldn't stop us from being together. She had no power over us.

Jonah glanced at the large clock mounted over the doors then frowned. "I've got to go. I got a transmit this morning ordering me to the office."

"Why? What is it?" I tried not to sound worried for his sake, but my voice hit a shrill note.

"I don't know, but it's serious. They asked for my parents to come, too. Can you believe it? They didn't even check the records."

Jonah's father had been exiled from Dawn for an illegal gen-eng procedure. Sent into the Beyond. A terrible punishment. He was diabetic and had just gone in for an implant of insulin-producing cells. Jonah had said his father didn't know they'd done a gen-eng procedure instead, until it was too late.

"Where's your mother?" I looked around. If I was going to meet her, I didn't want to make a bad impression – we'd had enough of that.

"She has to work."

"Well, they probably just want to congratulate you on your work in the lab," I said, trying to convince us both.

"Yeah, right." Jonah laughed. "Whatever it is, I'm not going to be late."

"You're never late. You always work hard. I'm sure it will be good news," I said. Jonah dealt with the disgrace of his father by constantly proving his worth.

He swept his fingers up and down my arm and I shivered.

"I hope so." Then he was gone.

I headed for my first class, a required course in creative thinking that my professor liked to call Creative Thunk. I liked Professor Fwatt's class almost as much as the few art classes that I got each month. They were just token classes where we accurately reproduced still images or created advertisements to promote Purity, yet I was pathetically grateful for them.

Near the entrance to Fwatt's room, Jobey Mendleson and a few others were gathered in a circle.

"Don't get too close. It may be catching," Jobey said with a snorting laugh.

The other guys only came up to Jobey's shoulders. His arm muscles were hardly contained by his uniform.

I tried to peer between them. Which sniveling first-year had they cornered now?

I gasped. It was that poor game junky, his cheeks burning so red that his freckles had disappeared. They had him surrounded, although he looked ready to dive out of his wheelchair and smash his fist into Jobey's stomach.

"Move, you gorilla. Go get your intelligence supplements." He rolled his chair forward as if he were going to run Jobey down.

Jobey pulled back his fist, his face dark with fury. "What did you say?"

"Leave off, Jobey." My mouth was as dry as cotton. What was I doing? I didn't even know this guy.

Jobey turned to glare at me, his fist still poised. The tight circle widened. I swallowed, not daring to take my eyes off Jobey's fist. *Please, don't hit me.*

A hand on my shoulder made me jump. Professor Fwatt. I let out a breath.

"Ah, a situation. Thank you, Mr. Mendleson for your kind treatment of our new student. We'll talk about this after class, shall we?"

Jobey lowered his fist, but his face grew redder. He glowered at me as if it were my fault.

Fwatt turned to the game junky. Jobey and his guys scattered. "You must be Reginald Gray." He smiled, and thick wrinkles sprouted around his eyes.

The professor was ancient with a small, round belly. He wore a shabby, dark-blue instructor's uniform that he'd probably gotten years ago when he first became a professor.

"Redge," said the game junky in a gruff voice.

"Pardon?" The professor's smile faded.

"My name is Redge."

"Oh, of course." His smile reappeared even stronger. "Come. I've got a special place for you."

Fwatt entered the lecture hall with Redge behind him. Jobey lingered in the corridor with his guys.

"I hear he's been locked up in the medical unit," Jobey said, "but there's no fixing him."

"Why'd they let him out?"

"Don't know." Jobey frowned at me. "But we'll send him back."

I hurried after Redge.

The lecture hall had a stepped floor with rows of chairs on each level that overlooked a podium and display screen with the Academy logo swirling on it. Professor Fwatt arranged a space at the front near the left aisle that was wide enough to fit a wheelchair. Redge looked at it, scowled, then backed his chair into the space.

I always sat near the back, where I could fade into the crowd. Today, something made me sit beside Redge. He was misunderstood, just like me, and I was curious.

I opened my bag and got out my slate. Sitting in the front row made me squirm — it was too close to Fwatt and people could spy on me from behind. There would be no idle sketching during the lecture today.

Redge lowered a foldout slate onto his lap. "Thanks for standing up for me out in the hall." His face was still flushed, as if thanking me was an effort he didn't want to make.

"Sure." Should I mention that I saw him at the café? I wondered again what he had overheard me saying to Jonah. Maybe it didn't matter. Purity hadn't been following me, Mother had. When he turned away, I glanced at his skinny legs. Weird, but he couldn't be dangerous if Purity had allowed him to come here.

"Reginald," began Fwatt.

"I said my name is Redge." His face got redder.

"Yes, well, Redge. I begin each class with a discussion of the readings. I won't expect you to be an expert today, but you can skim through the topics before class begins. I'm transmitting now."

Redge nodded, then touched his slate to power up his knowledge pilot. He still had several bandages on his fingertips.

"Dawg?" Redge spoke softly into his slate.

"Bark, bark." The voice that answered was metallic – a pathetic dog imitation.

"Your pilot has voice commands? And a name?" I leaned closer.

Everybody had a pilot program with an agenda, assignment manager, and so on, but mine was nothing like his.

Redge smiled for the first time. "Yeah, listen. Dawg, a Chihuahua. Go."

"Yip, yip." The voice became a high-pitched yelp.

"I'd give him a biscuit if he had teeth." Redge's voice was proud.

"Ha, ha." The deep male pilot voice was sardonic now. "As your knowledge pilot, I'm obligated to tell you that I'm capable of more."

"Pure! A pilot with personality. How did you get that?"

"I modified his interaction program." Redge passed his fingers, wide and flattened on the tips, over the monitor as if he were stroking a dog. The fingernails that weren't bandaged were short, bitten back to the skin. "A Great Dane. Go."

"Ar-orf, ar-orf."

I laughed. "Amazing."

"Thanks."

Then Professor Fwatt began his introductory speech. "Please welcome our newest student, Reginald Gray."

"It's Redge." Redge muttered, shaking his head. He didn't take his eyes off his pilot.

"Reginald is a special guest of the Academy during his stay at the main medical unit. I expect everyone to give him a warm welcome."

The room was so silent that I could almost hear the questions buzzing through everyone's minds. Why had Purity allowed him to come here? What was wrong with him? Yet no one dared to ask, and Professor Fwatt didn't explain.

"Now, on to our opening debate." The professor cleared his throat. "Should an artist be free to paint any subject matter?"

Still wondering about Redge, I accessed my own, rather ordinary, pilot. I tried to listen to what the professor was saying, but I couldn't help but notice the sideways looks that Redge was getting.

Then Jobey entered the door at the front of the room.

"What if the artist painted the torture of children?" Professor Fwatt was saying to everyone, although he was giving Jobey Mendleson a stern look. A few people laughed.

Jobey ignored Fwatt. He stood with his legs wide apart and studied the room, looking for a seat. There was one in the far back row and one on the other side of

Redge. He glared at Redge, then scaled the stairs to the back, climbing over people's legs to get to the seat.

"Through censorship of art, we stamp a firm foot down on creativity and deprive everyone of the freedom of expression."

The topic was interesting – and daring, considering Purity's need to control – but I kept glancing at Redge. Why was he in a wheelchair? Was he skidge? The rumors about Jobey were that he'd had work done on his biceps, legs, shoulders, and a full plastics job on his face. If any of these changes had involved gen-eng, Jobey would be skidge.

"We do have a right to portray, in art, acts that are not permitted under law in order to provide a comment on society. Through art, society examines itself."

Thinking about what Fwatt was saying, I stared at the perspiration that was now sprinkled across his forehead like raindrops. More sweat was beginning to collect on the ledge of Fwatt's stomach and soak his uniform black around the middle. Many times I had watched Fwatt's race of sweat. I had even bet myself when the upper and lower bands of moisture would meet in the middle.

I thought about sending a transmit to Redge. "Fwatt needs to pinch off his sweat glands." I glanced at Redge, considering it. He was no longer scowling, although he appeared edgy, uncomfortable.

"Is the suppression of any form of creative activity wrong then? For example, should scientists be permitted to create a new species or alter at will the sequence of genes that has carried humans forward since our early evolution?" The professor gazed about him, waiting for an answer to this question.

This was what I liked about Fwatt. He had the audacity to ask challenging questions. I wondered how he managed it without Purity hassling him. Or maybe they did and I just didn't know it.

"What about lifeweed, Professor? Once we have created a monster, what do we do with it?" asked someone near the back.

Lifewort, I wanted to say, but I was frozen, waiting for the professor's answer. The stains from around Fwatt's collar were gathering strength now – straining to meet those traveling up from his stomach. I realized that I was holding my breath and released it. My father's creation. Was lifewort a monster?

"Destroy it," called out Marissa Francisco, a girl I'd once called a friend, until Mother had told her that I was too good for her. "If we created it, we can destroy it."

I wanted to interrupt, but didn't know what to say. Why did everyone hate lifewort? It might be invasive, but it had a purpose. It created the biodegradable plastic that we used everywhere – on the walk in the commons, in the benches at the Academy. Wasn't lifewort just struggling to survive like any other plant?

"Ah, Marissa," answered Fwatt, "life is different from art. Do the same rules apply? Once that life form has been created, should it enjoy the same rights as you and I?"

"Can't destroy lifeweed anyway," said Jobey. "It has an unbeatable defense mechanism."

I could keep silent no longer. "You're talking about killing off a whole species. What gives you the right?"

Everyone looked at me. Except for the sound of a shoe scuffing against the floor, all was silent. Then someone said, "But lifeweed is killing off other plants!"

"Ah, now we have an interesting debate." Professor Fwatt's face was triumphant.

If only I could wipe the glorious look from his face. "No, we don't. This is not a classroom experiment. *Lifewort* is a living thing."

"Her father runs GrowTech," someone behind me whispered.

"Ohh," was the answer.

This had nothing to do with Dad. How dare they gossip about me?

Then Redge folded back his slate, unlocked his wheels, and began to roll himself out of the room. I saw that Redge's face was red again. Maybe even redder than before. With one push of his arms he was halfway to the door. Where was he going?

"Reginald?" asked the professor, confused.

The class snuffled and giggled. This interruption was better than any lecture. Everyone sat up and paid attention.

"I don't belong here," Redge spoke with clear pauses like bullets between each word.

"Pardon?"

"You think you can just sit around here and decide what has a right to live?" The words exploded out of him. "I don't want to be part of this."

Redge avoided my eyes, but I felt I finally had an ally.

"Uh, perhaps you should go to the office?"

"Right away." Redge almost spat the words out. Then with two more strong pushes he was through the door.

Someone muffled a loud guffaw and the sound echoed through the room. Softer laughter followed.

The professor began to discuss how a society forms its moral values, but I was wondering where Redge would go. Not to the office, obviously. If only I had the nerve to follow him out of the lecture hall. If only I didn't have to do what everyone expected of me. I sighed and tried to pay attention. If only I could just walk out of the Academy without Mother hounding me.

purity

"How could you? You . . . you . . ." No name was evil enough to call Mother. "How could you possibly?"

"What choice did I have?" Mother's tight smile was infuriating. "That boy was a disruptive influence. Even though I forbade you to see him, the other girls at the Academy were still at risk. It was my responsibility as a parent to let the Academy know about the situation." Mother casually clipped a droopy blossom from a hibiscus.

Seething, I thumped down onto a chair. The forest of Mother's plants dominated the sunroom. They cast a shadow over me. Even the sun couldn't shine under Mother's spell. I should have known she would do something. I clenched my jaw. Why hadn't I been more careful?

Before me, the neatly set table grated on my nerves. I wanted to swipe the supper dishes onto the floor, hear the satisfying crash, and watch Mother jump. But

Elyle would just give me a disappointed look and set the table again.

"I can't believe you had Jonah expelled!" My voice was almost a shriek. "What about his job in the lab? His hopes for a posting? Gone! Because of you!"

"He did it to himself," Mother shrugged. "His genetic history is less than satisfactory."

My mouth hung open. Had she researched his family history? "You mean his dad?" I shook my head, amazed she could slur Jonah without a second thought. "That was an accident! Jonah wasn't affected."

Elyle appeared in the kitchen doorway with a huge bowl of spinach salad in her hands. A sculpture standing strong against the violent emotions that threatened to swamp me. She smiled sadly. I'm sorry, her expression said.

Why didn't she do something? Couldn't she influence Mother? Maybe Dad could fix it.

"Dad," I spun on him, pleading fast, "you've got to tell the Academy it was a mistake. That Mother misunderstood the situation. Please, we've got to help Jonah. He's a good guy, and he . . . likes science, like you do." Tears threatened to flood my eyes, but I blinked them back.

Dad folded his arms across his chest, his face grim. He sat in a corner, where the leaves of a robust fig tree dwarfed him. "Lenni, your mother did what she thought was right, and this Jonah has lured you away from classes . . . ."

I couldn't listen. "It was nothing like that! Jonah didn't want me to miss school. I did that myself." My chest tightened and the tears came. I glared at Dad, furiously wiping my wet cheeks, refusing to weaken. "You don't know what it's like around here. I feel like I can't breathe sometimes."

"Honey," Dad stood and crossed the room. I let him pull me into a gentle squeeze. His shirt smelled like my childhood bedtime stories. I leaned against him, rubbing my eyes until they hurt. "It's for the best," he whispered into my hair. "His father was exiled."

I stiffened, then pulled away. "So you knew about this?"

His eyes widened, surprised.

"You knew? And you didn't stop her?"

Elyle walked to the table and set down the bowl. A waft of onion and garlic circled my head. Fresh, crisp spinach leaves in a room of decay.

"I didn't know what your mother had planned," Dad began, "but I can't say I disagree with her. From what I've heard . . ."

"From what you've heard?" I screamed, shaking now. "Did you ask me? Consider where you got your information, Dad." I pointed at Mother. "She lies."

"Calm down, Lenni." Dad patted my shoulder but I jerked away. He glanced questioningly at Mother. "Are you saying his father wasn't exiled?"

"Well, no." I admitted, flustered. "He was. But Jonah wasn't."

Mother sniffed. "You don't want to dilute your genetic heritage with someone like him. You have a responsibility to the future."

"What?"

"Lenni!" Elyle's voice was a warning. Don't get Mother upset.

"Don't, Elyle!" I whirled violently to face her, smashing into a chair, sending it clattering across the floor. "How can you do nothing? How can you let her get away with this?"

Elyle froze, staring at me. Why had I attacked her? I rubbed my swollen eyes and glanced away. My face was hot; my head spinning.

"All these secrets you keep, Lenni." Mother's voice was smug as she clipped another flower. "Sneaking around with that boy. And those ghastly portraits."

I stepped back with a jolt and bumped into the fallen chair. "Don't insult my portraits!" I screeched at her.

"Why do you draw such dreadful pictures? And I hear you were charging for them like a beggar girl. It will have to stop."

"Do you know every move I make?" I turned to Dad, desperate. "Please. Don't you see what she's doing? My life's a prison."

Dad rubbed his neck. His cheeks were flushed, and his eyebrows furrowed. "What do you want me to do?" His eyes flickered over Mother then away, his shoulders slumped, and I knew. He was just as stuck as I was.

"Oh, Dad." I sighed. Jonah. My portraits. Everything taken away. And no one to help.

Just then, a knock came at the front door. Dad dashed for the hall.

"Dad!"

"Later, Lenni."

I stomped down the hall after him. "Dad!"

He opened the front door and the sweltering heat rushed in. Two Purity officers stood on the step. My stomach lurched. Bulky men with thick necks. They were here for me at last. That woman had reported me. Sour bile rose into my mouth.

"Mr. Leonard Hannix?" The taller man asked.

"Yes?" Dad held the doorknob in a tight grip.

"We need you to come with us."

I swallowed, leaned against the wall for support. Dad? They wanted my father? What could Purity want with him?

Mother shuffled down the hall with Elyle behind.

"Who is it, Leonard?" She pushed past me, but Dad moved to block her view.

"Nothing to worry about, Mara." His voice was deadpan. "Elyle, please see to my wife. This doesn't concern her."

"Just a few questions for your husband, Ms. Hannix," said the other officer.

Mother peered around Dad and caught a glimpse of the officers. She gasped. "You're from Purity!"

"Yes."

Their badges were pinned to their chests, gleaming with some secret purpose. Genetic Purity Council. What would they do to Dad?

"What is it about?" Mother's hand shook as she raised it to her throat.

"Lifewort, of course." Dad's voice was falsely calm.

"Is it?" She trembled, grabbing my arm for support.

"Get off," I muttered, shaking free of her.

"Yes, Mara." Dad glanced uneasily at Mother.

"Are you sure?" Mother's rolling chins had a jelly-like quiver that I'd never seen.

"Yes. Elyle, now, please." Dad reached for his shoes. Then to the officers he said, "My wife has delicate health."

"It's not about . . ."

"No, Mara." Dad's look sliced off her words.

Mother was babbling nonsense again — it was our typical sickening family drama. Elyle grabbed Mother by the wrist, but she twisted away. The crowd of bodies in the hall flattened me against the wall. I slid into the doorway of the living room.

"What about lifewort?" Mother pushed past Dad. "Leonard did nothing wrong."

The officers showed no emotion. "Like I said, Ms. Hannix," began the second officer, "just a few questions."

"Mara!" Elyle tugged at her.

"I demand that . . ." Mother began.

"Enough, Mara," Dad barked.

Mother shut her mouth.

My heartbeats filled the silence. Dad had finally found a voice against Mother. Why couldn't he stand up for me?

"Just a few questions," repeated the Purity officer.

"Mara needs to lie down, Elyle." Dad had his shoes on, but they were untied. He rushed out the door, then slammed it.

I hurried to the front window to watch Dad go. The Purity officers walked on either side of him, as if they thought he might try to escape. They opened the door of a small silver car. Dad couldn't protect me from Mother now, even if he wanted to.

"Will they take him to Detention Block?" I asked, suddenly concerned. "Will he be all right? How long will he be gone?"

Elyle was still in the hall, probably trying to prod Mother away from the door.

Mother's frantic voice burst out. "Lenni, where's Lenni?"

What did she want now? I had no desire to see her ever again. I fingered my waterstone in my pocket. It didn't seem to be guarding me from anything.

"Hush. She's fine. In the front room." Elyle soothed her with a quiet, singsong voice.

"Where? I need to see her."

"Hush. To bed with you, Mara. Time to rest."

"No."

"Come, Mara."

"I need to see Lenni." Her voice had that shrill tone again.

"You're tired. Come upstairs."

"No."

A crash like the sound of a huge wave thundering against rock came from the hall.

"Lenni," Elyle called. "I need you!"

I dashed for the hall and gasped. Elyle was bent over Mother. Mother lay sprawled across the floor with her head resting on the bottom shelf in the closet, a deep gash in her forehead dripping blood onto the mat.

"Ohh." Mother didn't open her eyes.

She was hurt this time, lying beached and helpless. How could she make me feel sorry for her when she was the one on attack?

"Help me get her to the couch," said Elyle. "Hurry. We may need to call the doctor."

I rushed to obey.

fighting indigo

Elyle trailed me across the main hall of the Academy. I could feel my face burning with embarrassment. I walked faster to leave her behind.

"Lenni! Can we talk?"

My jaw tightened. Was she going to walk me to class?

Go home, I silently willed her, as I started up the curved stone staircase to the second floor. *Go home to her.*

I'd been fighting everyone since Dad had reappeared. I was relieved to see him after only one night with Purity, yet I couldn't help but resent him, too. He hadn't even tried to help Jonah. Mother hadn't emerged from her room last night, although she had been alert enough to make Elyle soldier me to school. Mother was a constant presence, lurking nearby. She was ill enough to faint under stress, but she wielded a power from her bed that was strong enough to strangle the sympathy I had for her.

"Lenni?"

"I can't be late," I said through my teeth. Somehow, Elyle's efforts to help made it worse. Mother had sent her. Mother controlled everything.

I tried not to stomp up each step. People were already staring at us and I didn't want to make a scene.

"Let me help, Lenni."

"Help?" I was on the top step now and I spun around to face Elyle, my shoulder bag almost swinging into her face. "You could have helped last night," I hissed as quietly as I could. "Jonah doesn't deserve this."

"I'm trying right now. I'm trying to help you understand her," Elyle said.

That was too much. "Understand what?" My voice was caught between a whisper and a yell, and a first-year kid glanced over at me on his way down the stairs. "What I don't understand is how she got them to believe her lies."

"I mean understand her illness." Elyle's voice was calm, her eyes warm with sympathy. "Why she acts this way."

I folded my arms across my chest. "Listen, I promised myself that I wouldn't talk about it, or worse, embarrass myself at school. So just leave, and let me go to class like I'm supposed to."

"Lenni, I want to protect you. Explain why she has certain . . . anxieties."

"I don't need protection." My voice was too loud. Why couldn't I just shut up?

"Maybe you do."

"What does that mean?"

Now people really were staring. I even noticed Redge in his wheelchair watching from the second-floor landing. Everyone's eyes were on me as they made a wide path around us on the stairs.

"What is Jonah supposed to do now?" I continued, unable to stop the gush of words and the hot flush seeping through me. "Why should he get expelled because of her? How am I going to see him again?" My cheeks were sure to be flaming red by now.

Elyle reached out for me with both arms, her fingers extended, grasping for me. "Let me help you calm down. There must be a room where we can . . ."

"No." I didn't want to hear her reasons. I didn't want excuses for Mother's behavior.

Elyle's fingers touched my arm with a gentle sweep. I tried to brush her away. She reached out again. I pushed her hands hard away from me.

"Leave me alone." Each word was a boulder, thrusting her back.

Elyle teetered on the edge of the stair. With her eyebrows raised in alarm, she reached for me again. No, she couldn't fall! I stepped toward her, tried to grab her hands. Our fingers touched then slid apart.

"Elyle!" I screamed, willing her to stop falling.

She slipped backward down the stairs, her eyes fixed on me. Others shouted around me. I froze, unable to turn away, unable to prevent what was happening.

Elyle tumbled down, twirling and spinning. When her head banged the railing, her eyes blinked horribly shut. People tried to block her fall, but Elyle thudded on, until she came to a stop in a silent heap at the bottom of the stairs.

Oh, Mur! What have I done?

I stumbled down the stairs, slipping as I jumped down three steps at once, dodging a girl who had fallen, crunching over the pieces of her smashed slate.

"Move! Please!" I shouted.

Elyle was too still. One arm behind her as if broken. Her head thrown back and to one side.

Don't let her be dead. Oh, don't let her be dead.

I knelt beside her, a crowd of people around me. I listened for breath from her nose, from her open mouth, but I heard nothing.

"Get help!" someone said.

I squeezed my fists against my eyes to keep the tears in. *Mur, help me!* I had done this. I had to fix it. I had to do something.

The woman! Had I really healed her? Maybe I could do it again. I had to try.

People gasped and talked in loud voices. I fumbled in my bag for my slate, my fingers too jittery to keep still. I grabbed the slate. Powered it on. Closed my eyes, took some deep breaths, and tried to envision Elyle, as she now lay, broken at the bottom of the stairs. One arm twisted. Her head bent at an angle. Once I held the image, I reached out to find the energy that was Elyle.

Please, Mur. Elyle has fallen.

I am here.

I felt Mur's warm wind and the lick of sunlight on my face, then *wham!* I collided with Elyle's energy. It was thick and hard to penetrate. I pushed my way through the sludge, hating the clogging dampness, and finally broke through into a place of utter cold and gray mist. The air was musty and dense. Gray rock stretched as far as I could see, broken only by a winding gray river. It was a bleak, miserable place. It couldn't be Elyle's world.

Yet, there, kneeling beside the river, was Elyle. On the river's surface swirled translucent rainbow pools of light, currents of pale pink, yellow, and green. Elyle knelt on a rock and watched the river. She bent over and looked into the swirling light, as if searching for her reflection.

Elyle, I called. If only this were a dream. If only I could wake us both.

Elyle turned, stared without seeing, and returned to her search. She dipped her hands into the river and let the rainbow light play on her fingers. I could see color draining from her fingertips and swirling down into the water.

I lost something, she said.

I moved closer to her, wanting to sob, to pull her to me, and burst free from this place. *I'll help you.*

Elyle ignored me.

I inhaled the thick, muggy air. I had to draw Elyle, not as this lost fragile creature, but Elyle as I knew she could be. In this silent, dull place, I reached for her, aware that in that other place, I was sketching her on my slate.

When I gripped Elyle's shoulders, I found I could hold onto her. Elyle softened into the pressure and allowed herself to be pulled to standing.

I wanted to hug her and beg forgiveness, yet she looked so confused, and the light that was left in her body was so dim, so clouded. I knew her light was being tugged down into the river. I knew she was dying, but I couldn't let her go. I had pushed her. I had to pull her back. I kept drawing Elyle as I wanted her to be, not broken and dying in this gray, miserable place.

I'll help you, I said again.

Let her go. It was Mur.

I can't.

You must. Mur's words held a warning.

No!

Mur was silent, but I could feel her disapproval.

Elyle's eyes shifted. *Yes,* she said.

I turned from Mur. She was wrong. I would heal Elyle.

In the gray world, I touched the smaller break in Elyle's right arm – the one that had been twisted by the fall. Its texture, its energy signature, prickled with sharp points. I stroked it until it became smooth. Then I tackled the larger break at her neck. It was a chasm of inky indigo shadow. I attacked it straight on.

Get out of here, a powerful male voice boomed out at me.

Something knocked me away from Elyle. Surprised, I let myself be pushed away. The voice was not Elyle's. Who – what had spoken to me? The indigo?

I approached the chasm again and it shoved me with more force this time.

Get out, it roared.

I would not. I began to explore more cautiously. Elyle's heart, first, pumping strong and well. Then her lungs, filling and releasing. Then her right arm again, which I sewed together with needles of light.

Elyle reacted to my touch. The two sides were battling within her — the older original force and the new invasive one.

I returned to her neck and began to pull gobs of indigo out of the chasm. It was cold, so cold, in my hands, but now Elyle was fighting it, too. I tugged at the indigo. It resisted, then released. Elyle and I were winning the battle.

"Lenni." I heard Elyle's voice from a distance. I pulled the last indigo shadow off her and returned to my body.

My eyes opened to the main hall of the Academy. People were gathered in a tight, hot circle around Elyle and me. Their voices boomed too loud in my ears. Their faces pressed in on me. My body was shaking and weak.

"Wow! Did you see that?"

"She's alive!"

"What happened?"

My slate was in my lap and I glanced quickly down to see what I knew was there — what I had chosen to draw. A sketch of Elyle strong and well, kneeling beside a rainbow river. I had done it! I had healed Elyle! I had pulled her back.

"Lenni," Elyle called again.

I looked down into her warm eyes. Her cheeks were rounded into a smile. She sat up and moved her right arm, the one that had been broken.

"Did anyone call a medic?" I asked. I wanted to be sure that Elyle was well.

People stared in amazement from me to Elyle.

"They're on their way!" someone answered.

"How did you do that?" another asked.

"That's some kind of boost!"

"Maybe it's no boost." It was Jobey's voice.

I sucked in a breath, alarmed. Would they think I was skidge? I was too tired, too weak to worry much about what they might think, or if they would tell Purity.

"Don't move," a girl told Elyle. "You've had a terrible fall. Do you remember anything?"

Then my head began to swim in circles, and a throbbing tremor started to pound within me. I shut my eyes.

"Are you all right?" said a familiar voice. I opened my eyes to a freckled face. Redge's face.

"Yes."

But as I spoke, a frightening sense of foreboding hit me – like something terrible was going to happen but I wasn't sure what. I tried to reach out for something, anything, to hold me steady, but my arms weren't working properly. Then I couldn't see straight anymore. Colors swirled. My head grew fuzzy. And the throbbing grew louder and stronger. Where was I? Oh, where was I?

"Lenni! Lenni! What's wrong?" A voice called from far away, but my tongue was too thick to answer.

A blinding flash pained my eyes. Then I could only see a bright yellow light, like a huge sunflower. It had vivid purple and blue edges with a veil of darkness beyond. As I watched, confused and amazed, the sunflower of light began to dwindle slowly down to a tiny pinprick in a starless night.

Ping.
The light blinked out. I was in darkness.

fire

Flames licked my legs, rising as high as my stomach. The pain swelled into deep jolting tremors, then fell like waves. I stood in a fire that burned but didn't destroy me.

Waves of heat wrinkled the air. Wavering faces in the huge darkness beyond the fire. Mother. Dad. Elyle. Jonah? Redge. Had they started the fire?

Another figure in silver robes that shook off the darkness. A woman dressed like a warrior goddess. Mur, yes, Mur would help.

Her hair was a billow of finely spun silver, her eyes the dark mysteries of shadow. When she spoke, I felt the soft, familiar breeze, so fresh, so welcome, against my searing skin. Step out of the fire.

My legs throbbed. I tried to lift my foot, but it would not budge.

I can't.

Trapped! I was trapped. I yanked at my legs, desperate to obey Mur's command, but I couldn't move.

Step out of the fire!

I struggled again to take a step, then shook my head, defeated.

Mur draped red satin onto the black earth beside my fire. Mother sneered at her.

Step onto this.

I can't.

Tears pooled in my eyes. Why couldn't I move?

She showed me a patch of blue ice, now in place of the red satin.

Step onto this.

I looked at my feet, licked by flame, yet unblemished. Mother, Redge, the others – their faces pressed closer, gaping at my misery. I wished them away, but they stayed.

I can't.

Step onto this.

Mur offered me a pool of aqua water.

I can't leave my fire.

I understand.

Mur offered nothing more. She didn't try to put out my fire. I couldn't step out. The circle of people pressed closer. Mur threw a spray of water over their heads and down onto my feet. A brief coolness, then the return of searing pain.

Mur gave me a sad smile. A single tear wandered down my cheek then sputtered into the flames. Mur turned and walked away. I watched until the darkness swallowed her. Then my tears flowed.

undertow

I opened my eyes. Where was I? I lay sprawled on my back as if I'd been thrown down. Every muscle ached and my tongue felt chewed and raw.

Bright overhead lights made me squint. I tried to lift my head up, but it fell back down to a soft landing. There were sheets beneath me. I was on a bed, wearing a too-small gown. Had someone changed my clothes? I shivered with revulsion, not wanting to imagine a stranger handling me.

Glancing around, I tried to prepare my weakened muscles to defend against further intrusion. As my eyes adjusted to the light, I saw only a harmless pitcher of water, a glass, and some sort of medical device on the table next to me. The walls were painted the deep burgundy of congealed blood, the ceiling was blinding white, and everything was infused with a cocktail of disinfectants.

A medical unit? I thought. *What am I doing here?*

Oh, yes. Elyle. The fall. The gray river. The indigo darkness. I'd healed her! Was Elyle really well? Yes. Then tremors had shaken me – a punishment for saving Elyle. And I'd had that unsettling nightmare about fire.

I watched the dust drift and swirl in the slanting sunbeam that spilled in from the large window. The silence was so deep that I thought of outer space and the dust that must float and spin there in utter quiet. Was I that alone? The quiet became ghastly, vast, and unending. Where had everyone gone?

My head began to spin with the dust swirls and my stomach to roll. When I shut my eyes to steady myself, sleep tugged at me, like a relentless undertow. I sank like an anchor into it. Minutes or hours later, I didn't know, I surfaced again, drenched with sweat, my heart racing. When the door to the room opened, I struggled to sit up.

"Elyle?" I called, hoping to see her well, just to be sure. A familiar face would be nice.

But it was a man of about fifty, a medic in a white uniform, studying a scanner. He glanced briefly at me, and I brushed the tangled hair away from my face. A stale smell rose from my body, but I was too tired to care. I collapsed back onto the pillow.

"Are you going to stay with us now?" the man asked.

"Stay?" The question confused me. Was I going to stay in this room? Stay out of the darkness? What did he mean?

The man smiled, showing even white teeth. At least he was friendly, and I was so glad to see someone, anyone.

"I'm Doctor Frank, and you've had a bad seizure. Still not quite with us, are you? You're in the main medical unit."

Right beside the Academy. That made sense. "How long have I been here?" My tongue was thick and swollen, my mouth full of cotton.

He sat on the edge of the bed and eyed me curiously. The mattress tilted with his weight. "Do you remember anything?" His voice softened.

"Yes," I said, noticing that he'd avoided my question. Maybe I'd been here for hours already, and he didn't want to tell me.

Doctor Frank squeezed my hand, then let it go. His eyes were pleasant – chocolate with specks of gold – although he had painful looking blotches of dry skin on his balding head. Couldn't he do anything about that? "Good. Do you remember your name?"

"Of course." Why was he asking me that? "Lenni Hannix." My jaw slackened long enough to let the words through. Pain throbbed in my head.

"Good. Now, Lenni, have you ever had a seizure before?"

"No."

"I see."

He frowned, and I wondered why.

"What's wrong?"

"That's what I'm here to find out."

He scanned me, checking my temperature, the response of my eyes, and other reflexes. I scrutinized him, trying to determine what type of person he was. He really seemed to care, to be concerned about my health. I wondered how much he knew about me, about what had happened with Elyle. Finally, he finished his examination and began to speak.

"The good news is that the seizure seems to have had no lasting effects, although I'm bothered by this unusual fever. No infections. No bio invaders. For the life of me, I can't figure out its source. As for preventing any further seizures, I've installed an anti-convulsive device in the back of your neck."

Alarmed, I felt for the slight bump just below my hairline. A nervous shiver ran through me. "I don't need that." *Don't turn me into skidge,* I thought.

"Now, don't get upset." Doctor Frank continued, patting my hand in a soothing way. "Seizures occur when there is an imbalance of electrical activity in the brain. This device regulates that activity. It's already halted a second seizure that began as you arrived here at the unit. We'll need to investigate why this is happening. In the meantime, you rest. If you need help, just call out, and a medic will respond."

"I want you to take it out." My voice was getting an anxious edge to it. "I'm all right. The seizures are gone." *As long as I don't repeat that trick with Elyle.*

But Doctor Frank just shook his head, smiled distractedly, and adjusted the burgundy cover over me. "Now, we don't know that, do we? No, I think I'll make the medical decisions here."

"But . . ." I was beginning to feel helpless, trapped.

"I'll arrange for a supper tray," he interrupted. "Please try to eat as much as you can. Do you want a shower or should I send in someone to give you a sponge bath?"

The idea of food sent my stomach into spirals. "No food, please. I'll shower later."

"Right, then." Doctor Frank turned on his heel and marched purposefully toward the door. I was about to call him back, to make my case again for removing the anti-seizure device, to ask him how long I'd been asleep, when he spun back around, his eyes fixed on mine. "Amazing how Elyle Brahan came through that fall so well. I hear she tumbled from the very top. Not even a bone broken."

I fought the urge to jerk upright. My heart hammered in my chest. *He can't know anything,* I told myself.

"Amazing." I knew I didn't sound convincing, but I wasn't about to admit to anything. The words of the woman I first healed still rang strong within me: *Are you skidge? Purity will be after you.* Maybe I could pretend the healing hadn't happened. No one would believe me anyway.

Doctor Frank was studying me with eager intensity – as if he wanted something from me. I couldn't really trust him. I couldn't trust anyone, ever, with my secret.

"How is she?" I asked, trying to sound casual. I knew I'd healed Elyle, but I just had to check.

"Oh, she's fine. Ate like an elephant after her fall. We're just running a few tests on her."

Elyle was well. I *had* healed her. My body relaxed a degree, releasing a tightness that I hadn't known I was holding. Yet, this doctor – what did he know? Our eyes remained locked, his probing and mine aching to shift away. Then the doctor and the room rippled in the air before me. Maybe it was the device in my neck, or maybe it was just dizziness. I shut my eyes and immediately felt the pull of sleep again. I was too tired to think about Elyle, withhold secrets from the doctor, or even worry about Purity.

"Well, you obviously need your rest. We'll talk more about this later, shall we?" the doctor said.

Then I heard the door click shut.

I could tell from his tone of voice that he'd meant it. I knew I should have been concerned, but my whole body throbbed. I'd been through so much. Healing portraits, secret meetings with Jonah, clashes with Mother, and fear of Purity – the zigzag path of the last few weeks had exhausted me. I couldn't remember the joy of drawing, the comfort of Jonah's arms around me, or even the pleasure of food. Pain and weariness haunted my every breath. I burrowed under the thin blanket, grateful to escape into the deep freeze of sleep.

unnatural construct

I awoke shivering against the damp sheets, wondering how long I'd slept this time. Struggling to assemble the disjointed thoughts in my brain, I remembered the doctor's disturbing comments about Elyle, and how I hadn't even seen her or my parents yet. Strange. Surely Jonah would have come when he heard – even in Detention Block they allowed visitors. On the table by the bed lay a tray of nibbled food that I didn't remember eating. How long *had* I been here? I tried to wipe the fog from my mind.

Then a fresh tremor assaulted me, halting all thought for a moment. I twisted around on the damp sheets to avoid the pain, before surrendering to it. The room collapsed in until the pain cleared. When only a dull throbbing pounded, the freakish bump on the back of my neck itched. I scratched at it, wishing I could just gouge out the anti-seizure device. Maybe it had helped, but I'd rather take my chances without it than be turned into skidge. Who knew what it might do to me? I had to convince Doctor Frank to remove it.

Sitting up only halfway, in case the pain crept back again, I looked around. The burgundy color of the walls was brighter than before, and the angle of the wall looked skewed. Was it the wall or me? I couldn't tell.

Another shiver traveled up my arms and legs, and I remembered Doctor Frank's words. *If you need help, just call out.* I wanted new sheets, although I wasn't sure I had the strength to stand while someone changed them for me. Better yet, I wanted to convince Doctor Frank that I was well enough to go home. Well, I would have to get up.

"Hello?" I said to the empty room, feeling foolish.

"Yes?" the voice sounded flat and distant.

I spied the speaker on the wall by the door and directed my voice toward it. Could they hear everything? Creepy. "Can you, uh, please change the sheets?"

"Someone will be along soon."

Half an hour later, I had endured a shower, put on a clean gown, and returned to fresh sheets tucked tightly around the mattress. I was just about to climb back into bed when a knock came at the door.

"Come in." I called, ready to surprise Doctor Frank with my sudden recovery.

Elyle padded in, shutting the door behind her.

"Elyle! You're . . . all right."

Surprised to see her, I sank down on the edge of the bed. She walked toward me, alive and well. Tears filled my eyes but I blinked them back. Her right arm and neck seemed fine. Her skin had a healthy glow, although the lines in her face had deepened and she looked tired around the eyes.

"Shh. I'm not supposed to visit you," she whispered, glancing over at the speaker on the wall. They could hear us, if they wanted to.

I wondered why she couldn't visit me, but the sight of her reminded me of the horrible moment when I'd pushed her. I hung my head, grinding my knuckles briefly into my eyes to stop the tears. How could I have done that?

"Oh, Elyle, I'm so sorry for what happened," I whispered back, examining the floor, my hands, the blanket – anything to avoid meeting her eyes.

Elyle sat beside me on the bed, patted my hand, then stroked my cheek. "You're hot," she said. I dared to look at her. In her eyes I saw forgiveness, concern, and something else. Her brows folded into knots that I'd never seen before.

"You are all right, aren't you?" I asked. We wore matching gowns, and Elyle had on plastic hospital slippers, probably made from lifewort.

"Thanks to you." Her smile pushed the lines back from her mouth and created two round balls out of her cheeks.

She'd forgiven me. I let out a deep sigh. "I can't quite believe what happened."

"You gave me a great gift, Lenni, but it cost you." She spoke in soft tones. "Do you know you had a seizure?"

"The doctor told me." We weren't going to talk about the push. Maybe that was best.

"Heal yourself now, Lenni. I know you can get strong. I want us both to walk out of here as soon as possible."

I nodded. I wanted that too, although I wasn't so sure I'd ever feel well again.

"Do you still have your waterstone?" Elyle asked.

"No, it was in my pocket." It hadn't done much good protecting me, but I still wanted it back. "It's gone with my clothes." I frowned.

Elyle looked worried. "I'll try to get it for you."

"Thanks. And my clothes? Can you get those, too?"

The door swung open a crack.

"Can I come in now?" hissed a male voice. "Someone's going to see me out here."

I recognized the voice, but couldn't place it. If it wasn't Jonah, I didn't want another visitor.

"Yes, Redge." Elyle stood, smiling.

"Redge?" I made a face. What was he doing here? I tugged my gown down lower over my legs.

Redge wheeled into the room, wearing an Academy uniform.

"You've got the wrong room." I forced my lips into a smile.

"No, Lenni. I asked Redge to come. He helped you during your seizure."

"Oh?" Redge helped me? From his wheelchair? How?

Redge colored red. "It was nothing much. I'd read about seizures when I was messing around in the medic files with Dawg. I just kept people back, made you more comfortable." He was whispering, too.

104

"I . . . I guess . . . well . . . thanks." I backed farther onto the bed and pulled the covers up over my legs.

"You don't need to thank me." Redge blushed deeper. "I've been waiting for days for you to wake."

"We all have," said Elyle.

"Days! How long have I been . . . ?"

"Two days. Today is Sunday." Elyle's voice was gentle. She squeezed my hand through the covers.

My head reeled. "I've been here two days?"

"Two and a half, really," said Redge.

I frowned at him. Why was he here? Where were my parents? Not that I missed Mother, but why wasn't she ordering the medics around? She wouldn't miss this opportunity to control the situation.

"Where's Dad? And Mother?" I asked Elyle.

Elyle's tiger-striped eyes clouded. She looked away. "They've been detained for tests, I'm told, and they're forbidden to contact you until the testing is finished. I'm not supposed to talk to you either."

"Why not? What testing?" My heart thumped faster. This couldn't be happening.

"It's Purity," Elyle whispered, frowning. "No communication until the results are in. They tell me it's standard."

"Purity?" *Oh, Mur, they've found out about the healing!* I tried not to panic, but tension gripped me like tight bands around my chest. "What are they testing for?"

"They want to know if you're skidge," Redge butted in, his voice quiet enough so only we could hear.

"That's ridiculous!" Why had Elyle brought him here? I was tired. I couldn't handle this.

"Sorry," Redge said, "but I overheard Doctor Frank talking with a Purity officer named Rylant. She came sniffing around after your seizure. That's what I wanted to tell you. Rylant is suspicious because of the way Elyle's fractures healed. She doesn't think it was a natural phenomenon. She's testing your parents' DNA, and Elyle's, to compare it against yours. She thinks you might be an unnatural construct."

Rylant — I knew that name. But from where? My head was spinning dizzily again, and his words hit me like a punch in the stomach. Purity. DNA testing. This was it. Purity was really after me this time.

"Lenni? Are you all right?"

I wanted to speak — to confirm what Redge was saying — but my tongue had become too thick. I remembered a long-ago lecture on the necessary restriction of genetic defectives, but it had only been a discussion then, not something that could happen to me. Even though I was pure, Purity could still detain, question, and test me. I could be locked in Detention Block, sent to a work camp, or worse — exiled to the Beyond. They could sterilize me. They could probably even kill me. I shuddered, just thinking about it.

"Are . . . are you sure about this?" I looked at Redge, suddenly registering the debt I owed him. He had helped me during the seizure, and now he was here to warn me.

He nodded grimly.

"Thanks," I said in a soft whisper. Thoughts whirled through my head. This was a painful awakening, like being stabbed by a hundred needles.

A clatter of footsteps from the hall made us all jump.

"We'd better go," Redge said with a glance toward the sound.

Elyle gave me one last worried smile. Redge circled in his chair, his strong arms spinning the wheels easily, just as Doctor Frank burst through the doorway, puffing and red in the face.

"This is a restricted room!" Doctor Frank frowned at Elyle and Redge. Two more medics followed him into the room. He turned to them. "Didn't I specify that?"

He'd known they were here. The idea chilled me. He must have been eavesdropping. Had he heard our whispering?

"It seems," came a gravelly voice from the hall, "that I will have to post a guard."

The voice was grating. Who was out there?

Redge, who could see through the open door into the hall, went pale. He glanced meaningfully at me. My chills deepened into goosebumps.

Doctor Frank's hands began to skate over each other. "I told them no visitors," he said to the voice in the hall. His eyes jerked nervously around the room. Everyone else was silent. I held my breath.

A Purity officer entered the room. I gasped. Rylant. Now I knew where I'd heard that name – at the café, when they had come for Redge. Rylant glanced at me. Her shoulders were back, her lips pressed together, but her eyes – they pierced me as if they could see into my soul.

I gulped.

This was it. Purity had finally come for me.

rylant

Purity was here, ushering Redge and Elyle from the room, getting ready to do their worst. I tried to breathe slowly, to pay attention. If I wanted to defend myself, I'd have to break through the terror that was paralyzing my brain.

"You can access the Academy through your slate. No need to fall behind on your studies," Doctor Frank was saying. Although his voice was firm, his hand shook as he handed me back my slate. "But you will not attend classes or leave this facility until testing is complete. A guard will be stationed in the hall. Is that clear?"

How could Doctor Frank be so caring one minute and so commanding the next? Rylant, who was standing next to him, obviously made him nervous, too — he was scratching repeatedly at the rash on his forehead. But he was also sneakier than I'd expected, listening in on our conversation. Was he Purity's pawn?

"Why?" I looked from Doctor Frank to Rylant, trying to keep breathing steadily and acting calmly, even if I was panicking inside.

"Standard procedure." Doctor Frank's voice had a warning tone. "Purity monitors all patients admitted to this unit. Anyone who displays unusual abilities gets tested."

"What does that mean?" I asked, daring to return Rylant's cold stare.

A glance from her blue eyes was like being stabbed by an icicle. She was small, compact — built to survive — and her flat, emotionless face seemed almost inhuman. I bet she'd had emotional inhibitors installed. What would she do to me?

Doctor Frank sighed and closed his eyes. "Officer Rylant can answer your questions."

They want to know if you're skidge, Redge had said. My chest tightened more. *But I'm not,* I thought. *I'm not skidge.* I rubbed the bump on the back of my neck, wishing it were gone.

Rylant cleared her throat. "We're testing to determine your DNA inheritance patterns." Her voice was harsh, husky, heartless.

Doctor Frank gave me a concerned look that made me even more frightened. Either he was a good actor, or he really did care what happened to me.

Rylant continued. "We've already extracted cells from you and your parents. We'll be comparing this against your DNA records to determine their accuracy — and your true lineage."

"I know who my parents are." I sounded like a stubborn child. "This is all a mistake. I can't be skidge." I pulled the blanket up and held it in knotted fists.

Rylant gave me a skeptical look.

"It should only be a day or two," Doctor Frank said.

"Until then," Rylant added, "you're not permitted to contact your parents or Elyle Brahan."

"Why not?" What difference would that make? I was suddenly sweating under my blanket, but I couldn't give up its thin protection.

"If you have nothing to hide, then you'll be free in no time." Rylant squared her shoulders, her eyes boring into me.

"This is ridiculous!" I could hardly wait for the DNA tests to come back. Then she would have to admit this was all a mistake and leave me alone. "You're going to confine me because I *might* be skidge?"

"The rights of the majority overrule you." Rylant began in a lecturing tone, not the slightest bit ruffled by my outburst.

"I didn't *do* anything!"

"Maybe not, but the public has a right to an uncontaminated environment. Look, I'm not here to punish you, just to protect the community. Until we know you're pure, you'll stay right here."

I glared at her, speechless. *I* was a threat to Dawn? This woman was not only inhumane, she was stupid.

Rylant put a hand on Doctor Frank's shoulder. "Now I need to ask this young woman a few questions. Some space, Doctor?"

A few questions! Was she going to interrogate me?

Doctor Frank backed against a wall. I was grateful that he didn't leave the room. He seemed like my only friend at the moment, which wasn't saying much.

Rylant opened the door into the hall, and another Purity officer wheeled in a trolley of equipment. There was an oversized helmet, a display screen attached to a small machine, and a camera the size of my hand.

"What is all this?" I tried not to panic. If Dad had survived an interrogation with Purity, so could I.

"This helmet," Rylant lifted it from the trolley with a brisk, professional manner, "scans your brain, beaming images of its activity back to this machine." She pointed to the one on the trolley. "It's quite simple, really. Deception requires extra work in certain areas of the brain, so we can determine the truth of your answers by monitoring those areas. The camera will record our interview."

It must be some kind of joke, I thought. A truth machine that worked? Dad hadn't mentioned this, but then I hadn't asked him much about his interrogation – I was too busy punishing him for not supporting me against Mother. If only I had bothered to asked. If only I hadn't been so selfish.

Rylant placed the helmet over my head. It was lighter and smaller than it looked, and it seemed to mold itself creepily to my head. I could hear blood pounding in my ears as it tightened. Rylant lowered a visor over my face. My breath sounded too loud, trapped inside. Through the visor, everything was gray, murky. What if

Rylant found out that I'd healed Elyle? What terrible thing would she do then?

The other officer fiddled with the machine on the trolley then aimed the camera at me. Doctor Frank frowned and scratched at his rash.

"Start the preliminary scans," Rylant ordered the officer. He nodded, and soon I heard a faint hum. I didn't dare move. I felt like an alien. My brain was in prison. My neck began to ache from the position of the helmet. The scans seemed to last forever. I leaned my head against the back of the bed.

Finally, the humming stopped, and the officer nodded again to Rylant.

"Let's begin." She turned to me. "You will speak only when directed and reply with honest, concise answers. Is that clear?"

"Yes." A tiny speaker in the helmet amplified my voice, and I jumped.

"Then let's begin with a test question. Is your name Lenni Hannix?"

"Yes."

I glanced at the machine. Lights on the front panel flashed blue.

"Good. Now answer this one falsely. Is your name Elyle Brahan?"

She did want to know about the healing. I tried not to tense up. "Yes."

The machine bleeped and blinked red lights. Rylant smiled. I flinched. Could this machine really tell when I was lying?

"All right. Witnesses saw Elyle Brahan fall. Although we cannot confirm that her fractures were caused by the fall, we have verified that they were made and healed on that same day. Can you tell me how Elyle Brahan's fractures were healed?"

"Not really." *It's a game,* I told myself. *Just beat the machine.*

Rylant grimaced as the machine bleeped and blinked red. "Answer with yes or no only."

I had to tell the exact truth. Did I know how I had done it? I took a chance. "No."

The machine was silent; the lights blue. Rylant seemed to accept that answer. I breathed a sign of relief, which echoed too loudly inside the helmet.

"Did you heal Elyle Brahan's fractures?"

How could I avoid this question? If I told the truth she might never let me go. I decided to break the yes-or-no rule. "It's just something I've been learning to do. It has nothing to do with Purity or genetic modification."

The machine bleeped and blinked wildly.

"The tests will reveal your genetic history. Answer the question. Did you heal Elyle Brahan's fractures?"

"I don't know what I did." I tried again, desperate to avoid answering.

The machine bleeped again, as if trying to make sense of my words.

Rylant raised her gravelly voice. "Answer yes or no."

No escape.

"Yes," I whispered.

The machine was deadly quiet. The cool blue lights made Rylant's skin ghostly. She beamed, triumphant.

"And Myrtle Hillsborough — did you heal the sunspots on her hands when you sketched her," Rylant glanced at her slate, "just over two weeks ago?"

Her name was Myrtle? And she'd told! She'd told Purity! What should I say?

Rylant tapped her foot, waiting for an answer.

"Yes." I had to admit it.

Blue lights.

Doctor Frank, who was sitting on a chair by the door, leaned forward. "Could you duplicate it? Could you heal again?" He waited, his eyes gleaming with hope.

Rylant forced a thin smile. "This is my interview, Doctor Frank."

"Yes, of course." Doctor Frank's excitement must have given him the courage to speak up. "But if we could understand how she did it, just think of what we could do!"

"Doctor . . ."

"Lenni, have you tried to control this ability?" He glanced at the others in the room, then put a hand to his head. "My rash. Can you heal it?"

"What?" So that was what he wanted — to learn how I healed. Couldn't a doctor heal his own rash? Could I?

I caught a flicker of the overwhelming power I'd been trying to manage. Who else could have healed Elyle like that — basically bringing her back from death to live again? It was awesome, and terrifying. And I was sure it had caused the seizure and the fever that still clung to me. Then the darkness and the flames that licked my legs. Mur, and how I couldn't step out of the fire. I hadn't talked to Mur in so long. Oh, Mur! Where was she now?

Mur? Are you there? I called out, ignoring Rylant and Doctor Frank.

Silence. Suddenly, I had to talk to her, just hear her voice, know she was with me, helping me.

Mur, please?

The dark burgundy walls of the room seemed closer, tighter than before. The helmet pinched the lump at the back of my neck. Where was Mur? How could she be gone from me when I needed her most?

Mur? I was frantic to hear her voice.

Silence.

Rylant was watching me as if she could read my mind, hear me calling to Mur. Doctor Frank waited with a question mark in his eyes. Could I heal? Not without Mur.

"No."

Blue lights sparkled. The machine was silent, confirming my fears.

I couldn't heal. I couldn't draw. I could do nothing without Mur. For the first time, Mur hadn't come when I'd called. I was alone. Suddenly, I didn't care about Purity, or Rylant, anymore. Drawing, connecting, healing – it had all felt so right, so good. Yet I'd gone too far when I'd brought back Elyle. Mur had warned me, but I hadn't listened. And now she was gone. Where? For how long? Nothing else mattered but Mur. I forced the helmet off my head and tossed it away from me.

"What are you doing? That's valuable equipment!" Rylant roared, proving she wasn't completely without emotion. She retrieved the helmet before it rolled off the bed and tried to shove it back on my head.

The machine began to bleep erratically. The lights alternated red and blue. I pushed Rylant away. The helmet crashed to the floor. I rolled over and buried my face in the sheets. Someone tried to roll me back. I made myself stiff and heavy.

"Stop," Doctor Frank called. "Can't you see she's had enough?"

"I'm not finished." Rylant's voice grew louder, more angry.

"Yes, you are." I choked back a sob.

The hands stopped trying to turn me.

I didn't care what Rylant said or did. Nothing could be worse than losing Mur. I pulled the pillow over my head and tried to block out the noise of the stupid machine.

broken

I couldn't fight off the panic. I called to Mur, but all was quiet. Where had she gone? For the rest of that day and into the next, my thoughts were a silent, ongoing distress signal. *Mur? Hello? Please, Mur? Come back!*

I sat still for hours at a time, terrified that this nightmare would never end. Then I paced the room with a restless, driven energy – eight steps forward, turn, eight steps back. I measured my confinement in agonizing detail. The bed with its metal frame like jail bars. The window that wouldn't open. The side table, screwed to the floor. The oppressive color of the walls. Medics came to check my condition then left again, giving me a glimpse of the Purity officer stationed in the hall whenever they opened my door. He stood at attention, obeying orders to keep me captive, probably only thinking of what he would do off-shift. I sent transmit after transmit to Jonah at his old Academy address, telling him what was going on, urgent to reach him, but he never answered. He was gone, too.

I desperately wanted to enjoy the freedom I'd so carelessly taken for granted. Maybe I'd find Mur on familiar ground – at home, the commons, or the Academy. Eventually I picked up my stylus and drew a few cautious lines on my slate. Mur was most often with me when I sketched. Maybe, if I drew, she would come back. Yes! Maybe I could call her that way!

On the bed, I curled my bare legs underneath me. My feet were fiery coals, even though my hospital robe was too short and breezy. Wishing I had my own clothes instead of this further humiliation, I made a few attempts at finding an image to sketch – Jonah, Elyle, even Mother – but the overhead lights glared off my screen, the intense burgundy walls distracted me, and Rylant's glittering eyes seemed to stand between me and my slate. I would never get a sketch started. It was true. I couldn't draw anymore.

Then anger began to swell within me. Anger at Purity for keeping me here. Anger at myself for pushing Elyle. Anger at Mother for every bossy thing she had ever done. I saw the anger as a living beast – a beast with a wolf's face, long, rusty-brown hair, and glowing red eyes.

I had to draw the beast. His thick hair. His bloody muzzle. I sketched a quick outline. Wrong. All wrong. I cleared the screen and tried again. Over and over I tried, but I couldn't find the flow without Mur.

I finally threw my slate down on the bed and scrambled to get up, restless again, my anger melting back into despair. My feet ached as they hit the floor and my legs nearly crumpled, but I ignored the persistent heat in my body and the cramps in my tired muscles and began to pace once more.

Mur was really gone! I couldn't exist without her. *Oh, Mur, will you ever come back?*

I was spiraling down, spinning into a bottomless whirlpool. Heat consumed me, my head still throbbed, and I was exhausted, yet unable to rest. Worst of all was the loneliness. I didn't want to live without Mur.

I have to keep busy, I thought dizzily. *I have to stop dwelling on Mur.*

But how?

I could read. My professors had sent reading material and special assignments to the knowledge pilot on my slate. *The Curse of the Biotech Revolution. The Techno-Peasant Dilemma. How to Bring Polar Bears Back from Extinction.* I'd wanted to erase the texts, but I knew I'd be responsible for them once I returned to the Academy.

If I returned to the Academy.

I hurried to the bed and searched for my slate in the rumpled blanket, eventually finding it beside the pillow. I brought the document list on-screen.

Just then, a transmit icon appeared.

It must be Jonah, I thought. Finally. He was probably desperate to see me, ready to comfort me.

The screen blanked, then the hairy face of a sheepdog appeared. His tongue was drooping out of his mouth, a drip of saliva dangling from it.

Not Jonah. It was only Redge. I was disappointed, but the ridiculous dog face almost made me smile.

His words appeared. *Coming over. You there?*

Did he think I'd be somewhere else?

I wrote back. *How? Guard outside.*

Not for long.

He couldn't get past the guard! What was he talking about? I doubted I'd see him, but I smoothed my hair and tucked the burgundy blanket over my legs anyway. Soon enough, the door opened and in rolled Redge. He had his desktop slate open on his lap, and he was wearing a plain shirt and pants. His fingers weren't bandaged and I could see the deep Blass scars. They looked painful.

"How did you get in here?" I peeked into the hall as the door swung shut, but I couldn't see my guard. "Where'd he go?"

"Shh." Redge put a finger to his lips and nodded at the speaker. "I have ways." He wiggled his eyebrows and grinned. "Dawg can get in and out of restricted areas in the medical unit's computer. I just reassigned your guard."

"You reassigned him?" I stifled a laugh. I was cut off from Elyle and my parents. Jonah hadn't transmitted yet. Redge began to be a comfort of sorts.

"So, are you all right?" he asked, his voice low. "From the guard, I'm guessing you're confined to the unit."

"Don't remind me." My smiled vanished.

"What did they do to you?"

I didn't want to remember, but Redge had helped me, and I guessed I owed him an explanation. "Rylant interrogated me." I motioned for him to come closer, speaking in a whisper. "It was pretty awful. Before that, Doctor Frank installed an anti-seizure device, here, at the back of my neck." I rubbed the awful bump again. "It's probably useful, but I want it removed."

"Anti-seizure device?" Redge looked skeptical. "Let me see."

"Why?"

"It could be a monitoring device to keep track of where you are. See? I have one." He spun around to show me his own small lump behind his ear.

"What?" A monitor in my neck? It was horrible! Disgusting! I lifted my hair and twisted around. "What does it look like?"

"No, it's not like mine. Bigger. Different location, too."

"Are you sure it's not a monitor?"

"I could get Dawg to check for you, if you don't mind him sniffing around in your file."

"Do it," I hissed. I probably didn't have any privacy anymore, so what difference did it make? Everyone knew my secrets.

As Redge punched commands into his slate, I began to wonder why they would guard me if I had a monitor. I wasn't supposed to leave the unit.

"Did they give you the monitor so you could go out to the Academy?" I said to the top of Redge's head. He was still hunched over his screen.

"No, I had it long before that." Redge looked up, frowning. Then he said, "I didn't want to go back to the Academy after that first class, but Doctor Frank made me. He's the one who arranged it. When he noticed how I rewrote my knowledge pilot's program to create Dawg, he convinced Rylant that I could contribute to society, even if I was skidge." Skidge! I had almost forgotten that Redge was skidge. "If only they knew everything that Dawg could do!" He flashed a bitter smile.

He had already been through this, would still be going through it long after Rylant's tests had proved me pure. How sad. "What happened to you?" I glanced uneasily at his undersized legs, and then at his muscular arms resting on his wheels. "Did your parents . . . ?"

"Parents?" Redge shook his head and his face twisted into a resentful mask. "Don't have any. I'm a ward of Purity."

Suddenly, I wanted to know everything about Redge. I had all along, really. What had happened to him? What might happen to me, if Purity got some ridiculous idea that I needed extended tests? I was almost too afraid to ask.

"You live here?"

"You could say that. I've been here a few months. Mostly I've been shoved into different medical units and work camps in the Beyond."

"The Beyond!" I shuddered. "I don't know anyone who's been to the Beyond!" I'd heard stories about half-human skidge who ruled the streets. How you could get a geneblaster and a false womb practically anywhere and make a new species in your kitchen. "What was it like?"

Redge shrugged. "I only saw the work camps." He got a faraway, pained look. "At the last camp, a guard attacked one of the more bizarre constructions. Febber, he was called. He had webbed hands and gills that breathed air. Impossible to hide that. There was this guard who bullied him and called him 'Fish Fodder.' Kept saying

'Only the people that God made should walk the earth.' Until the day he let Febber have it with his prodder." His voice got hard. "Then Febber didn't get bullied anymore."

Redge blinked repeatedly. I stared at him, horrified. Redge slowly recovered himself.

"I'm sorry," I said, knowing it wouldn't help. I threw a worried glance at the speaker, hoping that whoever was supposed to be listening was asleep on the job.

Redge nodded, wiping his eyes, then asked more quietly, "You know why the Purity settlements were really created?"

"What do you mean?"

"Well, you don't believe that schlock they feed you at the Academy, do you?"

"No! Not all of it. I mean, I know it's propaganda."

"But do you know the truth? Did you know that gen-eng of humans used to be researched by respected scientists?"

"Oh, come on. They would never . . ."

"Sure they would. With government resources, they were out to perfect humanity, eliminate undesirable conditions – anything from poor eyesight to short people. Any fetus with a risk of disease was destroyed. Not smart enough – destroyed. There were a lot of kinks to work out as they learned how to manipulate genetic technology. That's when the Purity movement started."

"I know – to protect our gene pool. They introduced laws to limit enhancement, to guarantee our right to a genetically pure future. Blah, blah, blah. I've heard it all."

"Wrong again. Purity wanted to protect the future, but just for select individuals, pure or not, that weren't a burden on society." Redge was ignoring his slate and staring fiercely at me. His cheeks were pink and he was obviously getting worked up. "They didn't want to pay for health care, food, and so on, for the twisted creations that were made by mistake. Oil and gas deposits had dried up. The energy freeze had begun a frantic scramble for resources. Purity's select communities, such as Dawn, were just a way to keep the undesirables out and the resources for the select few. I bet you half the people in Dawn are enhanced or the product of past enhancement. As long as it works or benefits Purity, they'll ignore it. Dawn and all the other Purity settlements are just intolerant, greedy states, serviced off the backs of skidge in work camps and undesirables in the Beyond."

His slate beeped, and Redge glanced down. *Just in time,* I thought. His face was now redder than I'd ever seen, but I guess he had reason to be upset. Not that I believed everything he said. Half the people in Dawn were skidge? Not possible. Yet I was beginning to understand why he was so angry.

"No monitor," Redge told me. "But be careful."

"Thanks, I will," I said, relieved. I was safe, for now, although I would have to watch Doctor Frank. "So how did you end up in Dawn?" I asked, still curious.

Redge sighed. "When Doctor Frank got out of Detention Block and got his medical license back, he brought me here."

"He was in Detention?"

"Shh! Didn't you know? I thought everyone did. I'm Doctor Frank's trophy." Redge's wide blue eyes were full of sparks. His thick lips were set in a pout. "He created me back in a lab at Dumacorp. Of course, he knew that most gen-eng of humans was illegal, although he would tell you that the laws are too strict. And he knew that if Purity discovered me, which they did, they would label me a biohazard, sterilize me, and pack me off to some work camp. As for Doctor Frank, he only ended up in Detention for ten years, but my sentence is more permanent."

At least I'm not skidge, I told myself. I could never be in a situation like Redge's. "Why did Doctor Frank do it?"

"With a geneblaster anyone can play God!" He spit out his next words. "Doctor Frank said he wanted a son, but I know he just wanted to see if he could do the science. What was he thinking? He had to realize that Purity was going to catch him. They always do. Now, he feels guilty. He wants to help. He wants to do another procedure on my legs. Get me an education."

Redge was breathing hard with the effort of keeping his rising emotions in check. With a look, I reminded him again about the speaker.

"I can talk to a machine like no one else. But every time I leave this unit, I feel like someone is pointing a big flashing red arrow at me with a sign that says FREAK. Those kids at the Academy just see the wheelchair and think *skidge.* They're all probably coded against disease and programmed with memory boosts. The perfection of nature." He shook his head.

"Can't Doctor Frank fix your legs?" I didn't trust Doctor Frank. He was too close to Rylant and he'd tried to get me to heal on demand. Yet he had helped me recover and he seemed to care when Rylant wasn't in the room. If he could help Redge get out of the wheelchair . . .

Redge grunted. "He can't undo the past by fixing my legs! He can't take away who I am – how I was created! I was just cultured for a kick. Let's create a kid with no legs, Doctor Frank. He can slither around on the lab floor like a snake – entertain us on late nights. We can even have Skidge Olympics, if we create enough."

The strength of his anger, his sarcasm, frightened me. "So you won't let him fix your legs?"

"I *have* let him fix my legs!" Redge hissed. He shoved his wheels against the bed in utter frustration, jarring me. "Regenerative cell therapy three times. Frank tried to re-grow the nerves in my legs but it never worked. Now he wants to try it again with some new injection and cell-bonding technique. He's talked about a biotech prosthesis as a last resort, but I told him that he's not going to make me into a false-legged cyborg.

"You know," he continued his furious rant, "I've never been able to feel my legs. Do you know what it's like to hope three times that you'll walk, to go through three operations, only to wake up with the same old useless, shriveled limbs?" He slapped a hand down hard onto his thigh. "I won't do it again."

"I'm . . . I'm . . . sorry." What else could I say? It was a terrible story. He could never get better, never heal, and obviously never forgive. I wondered what it would be like never to hear Mur again, then I quickly banished the thought. Would I ask Doctor Frank for help, just to get Mur back? I didn't know.

Redge's mouth was twisting as something new bubbled to the surface. He seemed to be searching for the right words. "I wasn't going to ask, but . . ."

"What?"

"I don't trust Doctor Frank's worthless procedures, but I saw you heal Elyle. I mean, I thought she was dead, but then she wasn't. So I wondered . . . well . . . could you help?"

He was asking me to heal him! I couldn't believe it. First Doctor Frank, now him. My eyes skittered to my slate on the bedside table. Angry and hurt, I wanted to roll inside myself, disappear into the heat and pain that I deserved for pushing Elyle down those stairs. I hung my head to hide the tears that were beginning to well in my eyes.

"I can't do much of anything right now."

Redge exhaled deeply. "Oh, sorry. I shouldn't have . . ."

"It's all right," I interrupted before he made me feel worse. "Looks like we're in the same place right now." I looked up. "But if I were you, I'd let Doctor Frank try again. Over and over again. Until it worked."

"You understand nothing." Redge scowled.

"Maybe I don't," I challenged him. "But what have you got to lose?"

Redge stared at me for a long moment. Then he spun around in his wheelchair on the smooth, silvery carpet, narrowly missing the edge of the desk. "Come on.

I want to take you somewhere." His eyes began to sparkle with a different energy. He gave me a sly smile. Something had triggered a sudden mood change in him.

"Where?"

He pointed to the door.

"Out of the unit? But the guard!"

"No, not out of the unit. Purity is watching you too closely right now. Not that Dawg couldn't do it." He grinned widely. "I go on walkabouts all the time. Whenever I need to get away."

"That's how you got to the café!"

"Yeah."

"But how do you get out? And what about your monitor?"

"I just disengage my monitor, release the doors, and distract the guards. Dawg is more than Doctor Frank suspects. He's an electronic life form. He didn't used to be. I made him live."

"No way!" I glanced at his slate.

"You don't believe me?"

"I do, I just didn't think it could be done."

"It can." Redge wiggled his eyebrows. "Dawg?"

"What is your bidding, masterful one?" Dawg's voice, from the slate on Redge's lap, was deep and resonant.

I jumped, terrified that if we hadn't been heard already, we surely would be now.

"Are you afraid of a little electronic life form?" Redge croaked. "Maybe it'll take over the world and get rid of all us humans one day. We're not that great a species anyway. Dawg could outdistance us any day." He turned to

128

the speaker and pretended to shoot at it with his hand, blowing an imaginary puff of smoke from his index finger.

I smiled, preferring him confident and happy to raging with anger.

He opened the door a crack and peeked into the hall. "Just give me a minute," he said when he was back inside.

"Sure." Just to get out of this room would be a relief.

Redge gave me another crazy grin. This guy was part maniac, part genius. Then to Dawg he whispered, "Operation Rae, Dawg. Execute."

duke and rae

The hall was empty. No Purity guard. No bustling medics. No patients. Just a long empty corridor with a shining tile floor and sterile white walls.

"Where is everyone?" I hissed.

"Shh."

No guard. The glassed-in medic station was abandoned. As I walked beside Redge in his wheelchair, I had the eerie feeling that we were completely alone in the building – until I noticed a medic in an office off the back of the station. She had her back to us and seemed to be reading a display screen.

When we were far enough away from her, I whispered, "What did you do?"

My blood was pulsing loudly in my ears. We might even get away with this. It was exhilarating, like pulling a prank on Rylant and Doctor Frank.

"I arranged for an emergency staff meeting. Dawg sent a high-priority message."

"You got everyone out of the way?" I laughed.

Redge didn't answer but his eyes were twinkling. He spoke quietly into his slate. "Dawg. Wheels are rolling. How're tricks?"

"All's well, boss."

Redge smiled. "Let's go."

We took the freight elevator to the basement. Redge couldn't do the stairs in his chair and I felt too weak to tackle six flights.

"So now what?" I asked as the elevator lights blinked. "Where are we going?"

"Nowhere special." Redge shrugged and grinned. "Are you hungry?"

The door opened onto a narrow hall with square overhead lights. The idea of food made my stomach juices curdle. I felt dizzy and faint, but I ignored it and pushed on.

"But you said we weren't leaving the unit," I said, thinking of the café.

"No, we're staying inside. There's someone I want you to meet."

"Who?"

"You'll see."

I wondered what the big secret was, and where we were going. The thrill of leaving my hospital room behind was fading, and I felt exposed in my too-short gown. I began to worry. Could I trust Redge? He could get pretty weird, and he had his own agenda. If Purity caught me, they would think that I was trying to escape, that I had something to hide. Maybe they'd install a monitor! I decided to go back soon, hopefully before they noticed I was gone.

The tiled floor echoed my footsteps. Redge's wheels were quieter. We passed gray metal doors every so often. They were closed, but I kept expecting a stream of Purity officers to burst out from one of them. I followed a step behind Redge, watching his arm muscles ripple as he spun his wheels, noticing that he didn't use the controls. Maybe they were too loud. Maybe he liked to direct the chair himself.

Then there was blue carpet on the floor. We turned a corner and the hall widened. I could see an open door at the end of the hall. Voices came from it, and the smell of spiced food, which sparked a new wave of nausea.

"We made it," Redge announced, as we entered a large room with tables, chairs, and a cafeteria counter.

Two people in wheelchairs wore medical gowns like mine. The woman had only one leg. I couldn't tell why the man was in a wheelchair. I sidled in behind Redge's wheelchair, hoping no one would order me back to my room or call a Purity guard.

Redge waved at an Asian woman behind the counter. He rolled over to a table, yanked a seat out of the way, and tucked his wheelchair under the table. I sat, too, grateful for a chance to rest.

"We shouldn't stay too long," I said. "I want to get back before they notice I'm missing."

"Just a few minutes," Redge agreed, obviously enjoying his freedom.

Near the counter, a thin twenty-something man with a long ponytail was holding the attention of the two in wheelchairs. "We have to fight for our rights!" He gestured wildly with his arms. "Show them they can't push us around."

"Keep it down, Duke," said the woman behind the counter. One of her arms ended in a misshapen flipper with two bent fingers where her hand should have been. I stared at it. These people were like Redge. I didn't belong here.

The woman came over. "Hey, Redge. You brought a friend." She smiled at me. "I'm Rae. You are . . ."

"Lenni."

Rae bounced on her toes when she walked, even though she was old, maybe sixty-five. Her gray hair streaked with black was caught up in a bun, her eyes were almond-shaped, her skin gleamed the color of creamed coffee. Something about her appealed to me, and I felt the urge to draw her – until I remembered that I couldn't.

"Hey, Lenni. What'll you have?" She pointed to display boards that were mounted above the long counter.

I couldn't think of what to order. My stomach was still queasy and I didn't really want anything.

"I'll have the usual," said Redge.

"All right. Lenni?"

"Uh . . ."

"How about I whip you up a drink? I like to experiment."

"Sure."

Rae went behind the counter and began to clatter bottles together, pour, and mix. She used her good hand to hold a bottle while she twisted it open with her flipper. Amazing, how well she could do delicate work. She moved with beauty and energy, and with no shame for her twisted hand.

"You're going to like her," said Redge, staring at Rae.

"You wanted me to meet Rae?"

"Yeah. And I want to ask her something." His cheeks flushed pink. "She understands."

"What do you want to ask her?"

He shrugged and turned a deeper pink. "It was something you said. About how you would let Doctor Frank fix you, if you were me."

"Oh." Had I interfered too much – told him what to do?

I glanced around the place as I waited for the drink I didn't want. The man with the ponytail – Rae had called him Duke – was still raging to the other two in wheelchairs. Duke seemed normal enough, even if he was too loud. He had the fuzz of a new beard on his chin, and he talked as if he were full of fire.

"No way they can push us around," he was saying. "We've got rights, too. They can't just go around sterilizing people whenever they want. They can't just say that this person is all right and that one's a weed. They have too much power. That's why we've got to band together. We've got to work like a team. We'll be stronger together."

I admired his courage, but his words made me uncomfortable. It wouldn't help if Purity found me here with this ranting revolutionary who was probably skidge.

I wanted to go back to my room right away. This wasn't worth losing more privileges.

I opened my mouth to tell Redge that it was time to leave. Then, as if he had read my mind, he said, "Purity doesn't come down here much."

I nodded. "Redge, I think we should . . ."

Rae returned with two drinks. Mine was tall, very blue, with two straws. Rae set them down, then surprised me by sitting with us.

I wondered what she wanted, but Rae didn't seem to want anything. She joined us in watching Duke and the others. *Maybe I should just leave,* I thought. Yet I needed Redge, and Dawg, to get me back. I'd give him five more minutes, then we were going.

I sipped my drink to be polite. The taste exploded in my mouth — a rich and sweet fruity flavor at first with a subtle tart aftertaste that almost made me pucker.

"Pure! What a drink!"

"You like it?"

I noticed that Rae's eyes were uneven — one larger than the other. They were warm, welcoming. Suddenly, I was terribly thirsty. I took a longer drink. The cool liquid streamed down my throat and into my stomach. It curbed my dizziness in a way that Doctor Frank's medicine couldn't. "Yeah. What is it?"

"I think I'll call it Glacier Juice." She smiled, and I found myself smiling, too.

We sat in silence again, until I began to feel awkward. I should make conversation — say something, but I didn't know what. Finally, I said, "Who's that guy?" pointing to Duke.

"The leader of the local cabal." Rae gave me the same mild smile as before.

"Cabal?" I asked.

"A secret group trying to overthrow Purity."

Redge laughed.

A warning jolt shot through me. "Really?" A whole new world was opening up — a hidden world of truth machines, monitors, and killer work-camp guards in the Beyond. I could believe almost anything.

"No, but that's what Duke likes to think. He works here — cooks and cleans tables — when he's not grand-standing."

"Oh." I squirmed in my chair and gave Redge an anxious look.

"Don't worry," Rae said. "He's harmless, although he has a lot of ideas. His ideas aren't always so harmless."

"Rae . . ." began Redge. Then he stopped awkwardly and sipped his drink.

"What's on your mind, Redge?"

"I, uh, want to ask you something. Doctor Frank, he wants to do a procedure. He wants to fix my legs. He's tried three times and he never gets it right. Something that Lenni said, well, made me think. Maybe I should try him again."

A long silence hung between them.

Then Rae said, "You asking me what to do?"

"I guess."

"Hmm." Rae turned to me. "And you think he should?"

"I don't know." How did I get in the middle of Redge's problem? "I just know that I would try to get better, if I could." *And get Mur back. And get out of this place.* I just wanted my own life back, however messed up it was.

Rae looked long and hard at me. "That's another story, I suppose." She turned back to Redge. "People who are sick often expect they'll overcome their illnesses one day. Sometimes it happens. Sometimes it doesn't. Doctor Frank is offering you a chance. Maybe he can make you walk, maybe he can't."

"I'm not asking you to tell me if the procedure can work," Redge said. "I know that I'd be taking my chances. I guess I just wanted to know if you think I should bother trying."

"Hmm."

I took little sips of my drink, hoping to make it last longer. The silence seemed to last forever. It was sad, really, that Redge had come to Rae to ask for advice. Yet with no family, and no one he could trust, what else could he do? At least Mother and Dad cared about me in their own twisted, controlling way. And I had Elyle and Jonah, too.

"After I was born," Rae raised her misshapen hand, "my father rarely acknowledged me. I think he pretended I didn't exist, which was easy with six kids around, but I used to wish I were different. Normal. I wished he would like me. Then I realized something."

"What?"

"It took me twenty-five years, but I finally understood that we're all imperfect. That we need to celebrate the unique flaws in each of us. It's a concept called *wabi-sabi.*" She pointed at a painting on the rough brick wall. "See that picture?"

We nodded. The painting showed the last moments of life of a flower with large pink petals.

"To me, it shows the beauty of the falling petals." Rae continued. "The flower is dying, yes, but the satin of the petals glimmers where the sun lights it. The earth is dark against the shine. That's beautifully imperfect."

The painting reminded me of Fwatt's rather daring lecture on art censorship. Purity only fostered stifled, controlled images of itself. Nothing like this flower, with its raw, haunting splendor. I was surprised they even allowed it.

"Is that why you don't have a prosthetic?" I asked, as I pondered this idea of imperfections being beautiful.

"Yes."

"Did you ever . . ." Redge glanced at her hand. "Did you ever try to fix it?"

"No."

"Why not?"

"My father hid me away. By the time I could have arranged to have it fixed myself, I'd adjusted to life as I was. It's part of me now."

"So you're not skidge?" The question came out before I could stop it.

Rae laughed. "No. I'm too old for the genetic games they play now. That kind of fancy science wasn't around when I was young."

Duke was getting louder again. "We've got to fight together."

"Duke!" Rae called.

"Yeah, Rae?" Duke's eyebrows were wrinkled together. He glared at Rae.

"Come here a minute."

Rae turned and spoke softly to us. "I've got to settle him down. He can get out of hand."

"I can see that," I said, relieved that he had stopped thundering.

"Duke, this is Lenni. You've met Redge before. Lenni asked if I was skidge," Rae said to Duke as he stood over us.

Duke laughed and Rae joined him. I was left out of the joke. They were laughing at me. At the same time, I could sense the depth of the relationship between Rae and Duke. They were not just casual acquaintances. The ties between them were strong and firm. They had an understanding that I could only glimpse.

"Are *you?*" Duke's smile faded and he pierced me with blue eyes so icy they could burn.

"What?"

Duke slapped me on the shoulder. "Did you think you were the only one in Dawn? There are others hiding somewhere."

I was speechless. He thought I was skidge! I glared, ready to tell him off, when he continued.

"Do you have any special abilities?" Duke leaned over, examining me. "Can you hear ultrasonic sounds or tap into the seismic waves in the Earth's core? Anything unusual?"

"I'm not skidge!" I raised my voice. "This is all a mistake. The tests will clear everything up."

"The tests?" Duke raised one eyebrow. "I hope they do."

"Are you skidge?" I challenged him. "What's wrong with you?"

"What?" Duke's eyes bulged for a second. "What did you say?"

I clapped a hand over my mouth, wishing I'd said it differently, but he'd challenged me first.

Rae laughed out loud then, and I relaxed a little, removing my hand.

"I mean, you don't look like skidge," I said. Duke didn't seem ill, broken, or even weak. Maybe he'd been corrected. "But I thought you must be, since you were talking about genetic rights."

"No, it's not me." Duke spoke bluntly. He wasn't holding a grudge against me. "It was my brother. They took him when he was only six years old, even though they couldn't prove he was skidge. I've been trying to get him back ever since." He noticed my expression of horror. "Quit gaping, kid. It's much like anyone else's story."

"Sure is." Rae nodded her head.

Redge glanced again at Rae. "So you're telling me not to do the procedure?"

"Not at all." Rae covered his hand with her flipper and I flinched. "I'm just saying that you don't have to be perfect. Either way, with or without the procedure, you'll never be perfect."

Redge nodded, but he looked confused. "We've got to go," he said.

"Yes, we do." I swallowed the last of my drink. The bitter aftertaste overpowered the sweetness now, and I was beginning to feel weak again.

"All right," said Rae.

I rose to leave, sorry to go back, but eager to get there before a medic came to check on me.

"Come see us again soon." Duke patted Redge on the shoulder. "I want to talk to you about my campaign."

"Give them a chance to breathe, Duke." Rae's voice was almost scolding. "They've got enough to handle without getting involved in your affairs."

"Everyone who can has to fight, Rae." I heard Duke say as we reached the exit. "We can't get anywhere by sitting around."

Redge smiled. I shook my head.

"Duke!" Rae said as we entered the hall, "You don't have to recruit everyone you meet."

who am i?

"So if they labeled you a biohazard," I asked Redge, "why do they let you out to the Academy?"

We were safely back in my room. I'd been surprised at how easily I'd just strolled past the medic station with Redge beside me. When I realized that no one had missed us, I almost wanted to keep walking. It had been hard to make myself return to the prison of my tiny, barren room, and I didn't want Redge to leave yet.

"Not all skidge are treated the same." Redge seemed eager to explain. His own room down the hall was probably as bleak and empty as mine. "You have a full reproductive classification, right?"

I nodded, sinking down on the edge of my bed, exhausted.

"Well, there are two other classifications — restricted and discontinued."

"Discontinued? Then the rumors are true?" My mouth hung open.

"They are. Purity finds a way to justify it." Redge scowled and shook his head. "They have no problem destroying skidge if they don't want a DNA leak."

Maybe I shouldn't have asked, I thought. Redge's stories were too horrific. Yet I couldn't help myself. I had to know what could happen to skidge like Redge, Duke's brother, and the others that Duke had said were hiding in Dawn. Was it all true? It was too terrible to consider, yet too terrible to ignore.

"The lucky ones," Redge continued, "get a restricted classification, like me. Restricted skidge are always sterilized, not that it would stop someone who really wanted to reproduce. They're expelled into the Beyond, sent to a work camp, or confined indefinitely — unless they can benefit Purity somehow. Then Purity bends the rules and lets them out with monitoring. That's why I say Purity is a joke. If they're so worried about pure DNA, then why let me out? Or are they just using me while I'm productive? Maybe they'll discontinue me when I'm older!"

"They couldn't do that!" I said, alarmed. I felt hot, dizzy, and overwhelmed.

"Sure they could." Redge looked grim. "I'll get Dawg to show you proof, if you want."

Then the door rattled on its hinges. I jumped. There were three loud raps.

"Open up at once," bellowed Doctor Frank.

I tensed, suddenly wide awake, wondering how the door got locked. "He can't find you here," I whispered to Redge.

The sky through the open window showed an orangey-pink sunset. How long had we been gone?

Redge's face was calm. He shrugged. "Too late for that." Then he said in a loud voice to Doctor Frank, "Whatever you say. Door open, Dawg."

The lock clicked. Dawg had locked my room!

Doctor Frank bustled in with his lab coat flapping. Two Purity officers filled the doorway. My small room became way too crowded.

"Hey, Doctor Frank." Redge sounded casual.

I couldn't speak. Maybe Doctor Frank didn't know I'd left the room. Maybe he just thought Redge had sneaked in. I hoped he wouldn't tell Rylant, or force me to have a monitor.

"I know about your latest antics, Redge." The doctor's forehead was creased and the blotches of dry skin now peppered his face as well as his balding head.

"I just wanted to check out this room." Redge stared him down. "I'm thinking of changing my accommodations."

Doctor Frank's face turned red, making the dry patches stand out like white frost.

"As a result of your actions, security will be even tighter around here." He waggled a finger at both of us. "Officers have been assigned to shadow each of you, and they will not leave their posts without a verbal order from Officer Rylant. Neither of you will be left alone again."

Behind him, the Purity officers looked bored.

"The jailer is tightening the shackles, Dawg. A monitor is not enough." Redge spun his chair exactly 180 degrees and stared out the window.

"I'm not here to argue," said Doctor Frank, his voice softening. "You know I want the best for you, but you have to follow the rules." He cleared his throat uncomfortably. "Return to your room, Redge. We'll talk about this later. I'll come by this evening, after my shift."

Redge rolled his eyes.

Doctor Frank changed focus abruptly. "Now, Lenni, you need to come with me," he said, his eyes avoiding mine. "The results of the tests are in."

He left, expecting me to follow him. The Purity officers stepped into the hall to let him pass.

I couldn't move. My legs were stiff, my arms hung weakly. The tests were in. That was fast. Even though I knew I wasn't genetically altered because of my DNA registration, even though I knew this whole thing had to be a mistake — I could not, would not, make myself follow Doctor Frank.

"Come along," one officer said from the hall.

My head spun in hot, dizzying circles. I thought of Duke and how he had assumed that I was skidge. But I couldn't be.

"You all right, Lenni?" Redge's hand was on my arm.

My eyes found their focus again. "Yes."

"Go on. Just get it over with."

I forced my feet to shuffle out of the room.

One flight down in another part of the medical unit, two more Purity officers in matching silver uniforms stood guard near the doorway of a tiny room. Inside, Rylant wore the same hateful uniform, as did several more Purity officers. Doctor Frank, of course, was in his white lab coat. In my medical gown, I felt unprotected, but that was probably their intent all along.

Then I saw Elyle standing off to one side and I rushed to hug her.

"Oh, Elyle, I'm so glad to see you."

Why had they allowed her in here? Wasn't she off-limits, too? Maybe Elyle's presence meant that all was well – that we would both be released soon.

"Me, too, Lenni."

I ignored the awkward silence around us as I held onto Elyle and buried my face in her shoulder, inhaling the perfume of medical soap, but no lavender. Elyle smelled wrong, and I wanted to cry.

Doctor Frank cleared his throat. Elyle pulled away from me, but not before I caught the look of dread on her face that made me more nervous than before. Something was wrong. Elyle was upset.

"Let's begin." Doctor Frank motioned for us to sit around the circular, polished black table that took up most of the room.

I perched on a chair between Elyle and Doctor Frank. Rylant and the other Purity officers sat opposite us.

A cold chill passed through me, then I began to sweat. My system was so messed up, so confused. The room was dry, and I thought fleetingly of Rae's soothing drink. The table caught the gleam of the harsh florescent lights and reflected it back. The white walls were a refreshing change from my burgundy room, but they, too, added to the glare.

Elyle squeezed my hand briefly under the table, then let it go. I took a deep breath as Rylant began to speak.

"We will be showing you recorded interviews with both Leonard and Mara Hannix. My officers will record your responses. Anything you say or do here will be on permanent record with the Genetic Purity Council. Let's begin."

In the center of the table, display screens were angled in a circle so each person could see one. Rylant's assistants each positioned a small camera – one aimed toward me and the other toward Elyle.

I wanted to turn from the camera. I always hated being watched. Yet in order to see the screen I had to keep my head up. They had thought of everything.

The display screen flashed and I saw Dad seated in a high-back metal chair with armrests. Two wide black straps across his chest and stomach restrained him. More straps fixed each arm to an armrest. The room was all white. A truth machine beside him flashed blue lights. A familiar helmet, like the one I'd worn earlier, was on his head. From what I could see through the face cover, he looked tired and old. His skin was hanging more loosely under his eyes, and he had the stubble of a beard. His eyes glared ahead at something unseen. His fingers gripped the ends of the armrests. He was wearing the orange uniform of Detention Block. Prison gear.

I wanted to leap up and free Dad somehow. Then I heard Rylant's gravelly voice talking from the recording.

Rylant: You've been interrogated recently about lifewort?

Dad: I've nothing to hide. Lifewort was approved by Purity.

A loud bleep sounded from the machine and the lights blinked red.

Rylant: Answer with a yes or no, please.

Dad (sighing): Yes.

Blue lights.

Rylant: I've reviewed that interrogation. What I'm wondering now is, were you aware of lifewort's invasive nature before its release?

Dad: It's not invasive. It's doing what it was designed to do. It was made to resist drought, salt water, heat, freezing, insects, viruses, bacteria, and herbicides.

The bleep came again, loud and harsh. Red lights cast a glow over him.

Rylant (firmly): Answer yes or no. Were you aware of lifewort's invasive nature before its release?

Dad (frustrated): Yes.

Blue lights.

Rylant: I understand that lifewort was made to be so invasive to improve the yield?

Dad: Yes.

Blue lights.

Rylant: Was it necessary for lifewort to be so invasive, just to increase the yield?

Dad (monotone): Yes.

Blue lights.

Rylant: Were you aware that a resistant plant like lifewort could become invasive?

Dad: Yes.

Blue lights.

"Why are you showing me this?" I asked. "This has nothing to do with me."

The questions were so confusing and repetitive, as if she were trying to trick Dad. I hated to see it.

"You were instructed to listen and watch," Rylant said, her voice cold.

I sighed, glancing at Elyle. Her eyes were shiny and her hands were gripped tightly together in her lap. She gave me a weak smile then turned away, her chin trembling. I'd never seen Elyle so distraught. What was going on? I stared at the screen again.

Rylant: You used standard issue genetic equipment to create lifewort?

Dad: Yes.

Blue lights.

Rylant: And this included geneblasters, growth centers, and false wombs?

Dad: Yes.

Blue lights.

Rylant: So, in fact, this equipment could be used to genetically alter a human?

Dad (suddenly flustered): Yes, I mean no. GrowTech wouldn't do that.

Red lights.

Rylant (ignoring the red lights): The DNA tests show that your daughter, Lenni Hannix, is not a natural construct. Could she have been created in the lab designed for lifewort experiments?

I gasped. What she'd said couldn't be true! It was a lie meant to fool Dad. I glanced at Elyle, but she looked down and away. A single tear trickled down her face.

No, I thought. *Elyle, look at me.*

She wouldn't.

I stared again at the screen, trying to breathe steadily. Why wouldn't Elyle look at me?

Dad (pale and shaking): I have no comment.

He didn't deny it. Impossible. It was a mistake. My face grew hotter. I felt I would faint or burst apart. My fingers gripped the chair. I didn't dare look at Elyle now.

There was a break in the recording. It had been edited. Dad appeared again, looking even more haggard. The helmet from the truth machine had been removed. He was slouched in a chair. What had Rylant done to him? I wanted to reach out and make her stop, to comfort Dad, to hear him say how I was pure.

Dad: Every decision we make is a gamble. No one can predict what will happen when we roll the dice with Mother Nature. Without science we would still be living in caves.

Rylant: Go on.

Dad: I don't regret what Mara and I did. Not one bit. Sure, Lenni was made to measure. If any father could guarantee that his child would grow up to be perfectly healthy, or smart, or maybe just a bit better looking, wouldn't he? At GrowTech we were already working with plant DNA. What was one small experiment with human DNA?

> *No, Dad,* I thought. *Please don't say it.*
> But he kept talking.

Dad (proudly): We protected our work. We avoided detection. We got her past the routine screening for health benefits and insurance by substituting naturally cultivated DNA. We tried to shield her from all this. Guess it didn't work.

> Was I just one of his experiments, like lifewort, another weed to be destroyed? I rubbed my face, trying desperately to clear my thoughts, to sort this mess out. How could Dad do this to me?

Rylant (still off-screen): What about Elyle Brahan? Was she involved in any way?

> I glanced at Elyle, accusingly. She was the only person in the room I could blame. Yet her face was so tight with anxiety that I couldn't hold my anger against her.

Dad: No. She knew about it, sure, but she didn't join our family until after Lenni was born. Until my wife became ill. My wife was always nervous that Lenni would be discovered somehow.

"Oh, Lenni," Elyle whispered, gripping my arm. "I wanted to protect you from this."

I shook my head. "Don't say it, Elyle," I begged. "Don't tell me it's true."

"I would have told you," she said, "but we thought you were safer if you didn't know." Tears streamed down her face now.

"No!" I pulled my arm away.

Rylant: And the people at GrowTech. Who was involved?

Dad (grim): They were following my directions. I am responsible.

Rylant (sounding triumphant): We'll need their names.

The screen flickered and went black. Was this really happening? I wanted to deny Dad's words, yet I knew inside that I was hearing the horrible truth. This was why Mother was always so protective of me. This was why she panicked when Purity came to the door. This was why she was sick with anxiety. This was why Elyle gave me the waterstone – to try to protect me from Purity. A sob rose in my throat, gagging me. Before I could get control, Mother appeared on the screen. Unlike Dad, Mother was lying in a bed with no truth machine in sight. Her head lolled to one side against a white pillow, and her arms lay flat under a pale blue blanket as if they were strapped down.

Rylant (off-screen): Your husband, Leonard Hannix, has admitted to genetically engineering your daughter, Lenni. We know you were involved. What do you want to tell us?

Mother didn't move, didn't respond in any way. I sensed she was at the end of a long struggle, and I hated to see it. I may have wished to overcome her controlling nature many times, but I never wanted to see her shattered.

Finally, her cracked lips began to move. Someone's hand appeared, squirting water into her mouth. Mother opened and shut her mouth as if testing to see if her jaw still worked. When she spoke, her voice was deeper, rougher, even than Rylant's.

Mother: I desperately wanted a child. We tried for years, but (a long sniff) I just wasn't able to. Leonard thought of GrowTech, his company. It was his idea. No romance. Just geneblasters, microscopes, and a false womb. We could have just gotten help with conception at a clinic. Then everything would have been legal. But the lure of gen-eng was too much for us. Both Leonard and I knew we would do it. He wanted a boy, of course, but I insisted on a girl. We almost separated over that, so I let him name her Lenni, after himself. We wanted her to be perfect. Tall and beautiful. Athletic and smart. Creative and sensitive. No diseases. High quality. But Leonard – he had a few undesirable traits in his family that might have come through in spite of the gen-eng. I didn't truly trust the science, so I had to take control. I had to get a better specimen to be Lenni's biological father. Lenni couldn't pick her own genes, so I did it for her. She'll thank me for that.

"What is she saying?" I had to interrupt. This was too much.

Rylant froze the screen.

"What do you think she is saying?" Rylant raised her eyebrows.

"I . . . I don't know."

Rylant ignored me. "Elyle, do you have any knowledge of Mara Hannix's actions?"

Elyle shook her head. "I was not involved."

"Yes, my sources confirm that." Rylant turned back to me, so smug, so satisfied. "Leonard is not your biological father. Your mother introduced another specimen into the mix, which we have yet to identify. But we will."

My head started pounding. I hugged myself and began to rock back and forth. Mother had arranged it all? She had chosen who I was? How I looked, how I acted, my gender, my personality? She controlled everything? And Dad was not my father?

"You may leave, Elyle, once the medics clear you for release." Rylant stood up and nodded at her assistants. "Lenni's parents will remain in Detention Block until sentencing. Lenni, you'll stay under guard until further notice." She stared down at me. "You'll be reclassified once we've examined you more thoroughly."

Reclassified? I thought of Redge's horror stories and began to shake. What would happen to me?

155

Someone put a hand on my shoulder but I shrugged it off. Elyle? Doctor Frank? I didn't care. I slumped over onto the hard, black table and crushed my palms into my eyes. I wanted to scream, to run away, to cry forever, but I'd never have enough tears for this much sorrow.

Oh, Mur, I called out. *Who am I?*

Yet Rylant had clearly told me.

I was skidge.

a visitor

The dream, my first since the nightmare of fire, left me sickened and shaking with loathing. In this dream, I'd held my arms outstretched, palms down, for hours, days maybe, until they ached from the strain. Holding them flat while Mother dug and poked, raked and tilled. I'd simply watched as she inserted tiny seeds into the holes she had made up and down my arms. *Just hold still, Lenni,* Mother had said, and I hadn't budged. For some reason, I'd placidly allowed her to plant along my arms, and I'd held them rigid as the plants grew, binding themselves painfully into my flesh, growing roots like tentacles along my veins. Until Mother began to harvest, twisting off a ripe tomato-like fruit and offering me a bite. When I shook my head, Mother smiled and bit into it herself. Her teeth were pointed like daggers. Sweet-scented pulp from the fruit splattered Mother's face and glasses. *Delicious!* She moaned as she wiped her glasses with the back of her hand, only managing to smear the juice around.

I closed my eyes and rolled against the wall, exhausted and repulsed. Even in sleep, I couldn't hide from the horror. My parents had betrayed me. I was robbed of my self.

For days, I'd hardly set foot on the cold hospital floor, except for washroom trips and medical tests, during which I was followed by my ever-diligent guard. I'd stayed huddled in bed, unable to move, my thoughts more tormenting than Rylant had ever been. Strangely, Redge and Elyle were permitted to see me, although they were no comfort. Redge had said they were listening to us, gathering information about who else might have been involved. I didn't care what they heard. I was ruined, utterly ruined.

Shivering with fever, I pulled the thin blanket up and dragged the pillow down over my head, as if it could barricade me from the hideous truth. Mother and the man who was no longer my father had chosen me, decided who I would be, how I would act. Did they think I'd be happier? I wasn't. Improved? I wasn't.

One question remained unanswered. Who was I supposed to be? Underneath all their programming, their interference, who was I? I'd never know.

How dare they? I'd never forgive my parents. I pushed the pillow aside and glared at the ceiling, wanting to do them damage. Throttle the man who was not my father. Strangle Mother twice.

Maybe I shouldn't have saved Elyle, I thought. *Maybe I should've let her stay in that gray place with the winding river. Then none of this would have happened.*

Yet I was the one who'd pushed her down the stairs. I'd made her fall. Either I'd had a responsibility to save her, or I was no better than my parents. I'd manipulated Elyle the way my parents had manipulated me, just because I'd pushed her. Because I'd felt guilty. Because I'd wanted her back. What gave me the right? What gave Purity the right?

I wanted to wrench the seizure-control device from the back of my neck. I wanted to wrench all my parents' alterations out of my body. I wanted to become myself.

I would choose seizures. I would choose a defective brain, a frail body, and a substandard personality. If I could, I would choose myself – whoever I was – however imperfect.

"Lenni Hannix?" A business-like female voice from the distant medical station intruded, reinforcing the constant lurking presence of Purity.

"Yes?"

"You have a visitor. Shall I send him down?" the disembodied voice asked.

A visitor! Mother and Leonard were in Detention. Redge and Elyle wouldn't announce themselves. Could it finally be Jonah? And Purity would permit it? I didn't dare ask.

"Uh, give me five minutes."

"Five minutes, then."

I scrambled into a new gown, wishing impossibly for some decent clothes. But humiliation was one of Purity's weapons, so I just combed my hair into a ponytail and opened the door for my visitor. Five minutes later, Jonah squeezed past my attentive guard.

"Jonah!" I breathed his name, like a secret too precious to speak aloud.

I'd so hoped it would be him. I smoothed down my hair once more, hoping I didn't look sick. Jonah was here. Finally. He would help. He always did.

Jonah smiled with only one corner of his mouth. *Strange,* I thought, yet I didn't dwell on it. His lips quickly distracted me, magnificently chiseled into his bronze skin. His golden-brown eyes, his thick brown hair — I had forgotten how startlingly beautiful he was.

"Whew!" He glanced nervously behind him. "I had to go through a full ID scan to get in here. And they say I have to go through cleansing to get out!"

Jonah would endure cleansing for me! "You came through that? I hope it's not too terrible on the way out."

I closed the door to the guard, who had turned to watch us suspiciously, then bounded into Jonah's arms. Familiar warmth filled me. I nestled against his chest and rubbed one hand through his silken hair, aching with the pleasure of being next to him.

"I missed you," I said, trying to forget that Rylant might be listening in hopes of uncovering more details about me.

Jonah wrapped his arms around my waist and swung me from side to side. Then he buried his face in my hair. "Me, too."

Yet something about the way he held me was different. Maybe he wasn't gripping me as close. I couldn't pinpoint it.

Then Jonah held me back, examining my face. "How are you, Lenni?"

"I'm fine. Oh, Jonah, I'm so sorry about the expulsion. It's all my fault."

"No, it isn't."

"Yes, it is. My mother did it. She complained to the Academy."

"One complaint couldn't have gotten me expelled." His voice was tense; his jaw clenched. "Someone else had to be involved."

"You don't know Mother."

Jonah stepped away, turning sideways. He fiddled with my stylus on the side table. Was he mad at me?

"I tried to stop her," I began, but he shook his head.

"The expulsion." He frowned. "That's why I've come – to tell you about my new school. Lenni, I've been on interview at the Academy in Current."

"That's why you didn't respond to my transmits. But Current?" My heart sank into my stomach.

"Yes. It's the closest Purity settlement."

Current was also the home of Dumacorp, where Doctor Frank had made Redge. "I know where it is. Two hours away by hovercraft! You got in? Oh, I'll miss you."

I tried to hold Jonah again, but he grabbed my hands, held them between us, and caressed them.

"Me, too. Are you sure you're all right, Lenni?"

He was examining my face. Tilting his head as if a different angle could bring me into focus better. What was he doing?

Then I understood. He knew I was skidge. He had heard somehow. I didn't have to tell him.

"You know?"

I waited for his sympathy. Jonah would understand how hard this was. He would help me through it. A clutch of tears waited in my throat.

"About what your parents did to you? It's on all the news reports. Everyone knows."

They all knew. I felt invaded. Other people wouldn't understand, like Jonah did.

Jonah began to pace the room. "Listen, Lenni, I can't do this. Current is just too far. I'll have to work hard to catch up. I won't have time to visit."

Then, I finally grasped the change in him. The difference in the way he held me. He was saying good-bye. Leaving me. I stared at him, stunned.

Jonah had always wanted to teach at the Academy. Everything he'd done had been for a posting. Being involved with skidge would hurt his chances. Destroy them, really. Yet he had admired my independence and appreciated my sketches. Couldn't Jonah, of all people, accept me as I was?

Jonah stopped pacing. "Don't look at me like that, Lenni."

"Like what?"

"Like that. Think of how hard this is on me. Do you know what they're saying to me?"

"Who?"

"They tease me wherever I go. Jobey's the worst. Someone even broke into our place while I was at Current. Smashed everything and painted messages on the walls. Skidge lover." He shook his head and began pacing again. "I don't even want to talk about it. My mother's going to move with me. She says I need to put all this behind me. Go to my new school and pretend this trouble never happened."

"Pretend I never happened?" My voice shook.

"No, Lenni. I . . ." He couldn't finish his sentence. "I need to be careful. Think about my future. Purity has been to see me."

He gripped my hand. I pulled it away.

How did I miss this? I had sketched him. Connected to him. Then I remembered the look on his face back in the café, when we first saw Redge. He had asked if I thought Redge was skidge, and his face had been twisted with dislike. He hated skidge. Even me. Even skidge he used to love. Jonah was no different from Purity.

Then, in that room under the gleaming hospital lights, Jonah wasn't so beautiful anymore. All the warmth he had once brought me vanished. Yet the part that hurt – the part that Jonah was breaking – loved him still.

I stepped back. In his sleeveless shirt I could just see my favorite part of him. The ripple of muscles across his shoulders, glistening with a fine layer of his skin's oil. He could lift me with those strong arms. Hold me. I'd so miss the perfume of him.

"I wish it were different. I wish you weren't . . ." He stopped, glancing down at his shoes. A long shudder disturbed his body, as if he was disgusted by the idea of what I had become, what I'd been all along.

"Skidge," I finished for him, wanting to spew the word in his face. Jonah was weak – too afraid of Purity to help me. I wanted to hate him for it, but I could only feel a huge wound slashing open inside me – the raw hole that his departure made.

Jonah left without saying good-bye. Without touching me. Only the faint musk of him lingered in my room.

I lay on my bed. Maybe it was the dull, cloud-filtered light through my window, maybe it was the depressing rattle of carts in the hallway, but suddenly I thought I would faint, I missed Jonah so much. An hour later, when Elyle came to see me, I still hadn't moved.

"I'm being released, Lenni." Elyle said, stroking my hair. She probably thought I was upset about my parents. She wouldn't know about this new injury. "I'm leaving to see Mara and Leonard. Maybe I can arrange for you to meet with them, too. You need to talk to them, understand why they did this." She sighed. "They thought they were doing what was best for you."

Talk to my parents? I never wanted to see them again. And I didn't want to understand them. Why didn't they ever have to understand me?

"Lenni, did you hear me?" Elyle raised her voice. "Are you all right?"

I gave a slight nod, saying nothing. I didn't tell her about Jonah. I couldn't. An ocean surrounded me that Elyle couldn't span. I was alone. I was skidge. Just like Redge. The rest of the world seemed ridiculous. Redge. Doctor Frank. Even Elyle. We were all doomed anyway, marching off to our own hopeless battles.

"I'll be back soon, with news," she promised.

I nodded again, too defeated to cry, too despairing to expect anything but the worst.

Then with one last worried glance, Elyle disappeared, just like Jonah had, over that threshold that I was forbidden to cross without my guard.

tested

"Try," Doctor Frank begged. "Are you worried about seizures? The device I installed will stop them."

The pathetic creature lay on the table, breathing heavily. I think he was a cross between a squirrel and a dog. Doctor Frank had called him a squog.

"I know that. I just can't do it." I couldn't bear to look at the poor thing. He was a reminder of what I had become. "Who made him?"

The walls were drab yellow, the lights shone bright, and the room had a chemical smell. I hated this lab and what it meant – that experiments like me were created here.

"We did," he said, a hint of pride in his voice. "In this very lab. Come on. Just one try."

"You have a false womb here?" Didn't he understand that he should stop these experiments?

"Only for use on animals."

Like that made a difference. "Why?"

Doctor Frank frowned. "Why what?" He sounded impatient.

"Why did you make him?" Not because he cared.

"It's a harvester." He spoke as if I should have known. "Squogs were designed to hunt for nuts, shell them, and return them to their owners. They can be trained to collect fruit as well."

"What about machines or humans? Couldn't they do the job?"

"Well, I suppose, but that's not the point. Creatures like this will be part of our future, Lenni. They're miracles of creation. Miracles that we brought to life."

I huffed. "What went wrong with the miracle?"

"Wrong?"

"Why does he look like that?"

I glanced at him and wished I hadn't. A bundle of limp brown fur with a long stringy tail. Scrawny, with eyes glazed gray. He was panting for breath, not moving but for the rapid in-and-out of his tiny chest. My stomach knotted. I looked away, down at the polished white floor tiles.

"It seems to have developed an asthmatic condition that hasn't responded to conventional treatments. Now, try it."

I wanted to scream. I was just like this sorry creature. "Why are you making creatures to suffer? Didn't you learn anything from Redge? From me?"

Doctor Frank jerked in surprised, then began to scratch distractedly at his rash. "Redge talked to you?

Well, he doesn't always see the whole picture. He doesn't see the possibilities that lie before us. How we can make life better for people like him, and you, if we understand more about genetics."

"Make life better? Oh, yeah, my life is so much better now!"

"That's not what I meant. If only we could have the freedom to research, to understand the full complexity of human DNA, we could do so much more. We could heal Redge and yourself. We could . . ."

"But you made Redge broken in the first place!"

"That was an accident. Everything should have worked. I won't make the same mistake again. Now, please, Lenni, could you just try?"

"I can't do it. Don't you get it? I've lost my abilities."

Doctor Frank pleaded with his eyes. "Don't you know what you are? You're something new, exciting, superhuman. If we could only understand how you heal, and tap into it, I could help you control it. We could heal anyone!"

My head was pounding. My skin was hot and clammy. I wanted to lie down. I shook my head and my vision blurred momentarily. I was too sick to sit up. How could I heal the poor squog?

Doctor Frank tilted his head. "You've heard of energy healing, haven't you?"

"What?" I was surprised. Energy healing sounded like what I had done.

Doctor Frank smiled then, like a kid with a new toy. "I've been looking into it since you arrived.

Apparently, energy healers are able to blur the boundary between the physical and the unseen aspects of our world. The interesting thing," he said, his voice rising, "is that tests have shown that a healer can send a charge of up to eighty volts through the skin to another person."

"Oh." Energy volts? I thought of Mur. Maybe she was from the unseen. Could I find her again? "Why are you telling me this?"

"Because you need to know what you can do! What you're capable of!" he exclaimed. "Exceptional healers can affect the brain-wave pattern of a person from a block away. Russian scientist Judith Chalikov tested one energy healer named Gertrude Borgough. Her brain-wave pattern was typically theta, the pattern associated with the state between waking and sleeping, as well as meditation. The tests we've conducted on you so far show similar results."

"So?"

"So! Just think about it! All matter is energy. Our bodies are energy. Energy is non-physical and infinite. Energy cannot die. It can only transform. You can transform it."

"I told you, I can't. I could do it before, but not anymore." Not without Mur.

"If we could only get you into a theta state. It should happen on its own. Who knows what you could do – who you could connect with."

For a moment, I let myself imagine that I could connect with Mur, that I could help that squog. Then reality popped the dream bubble. I knew I'd never connect. I couldn't.

The squog took another gurgling breath. It broke my heart just to listen. He heaved his head to the side and stared at me. Big deep eyes. I sunk into them. The squog gurgled again.

I had healed that woman in the commons without meaning to, and I had healed Elyle out of desperation and guilt for pushing her. A real healer would help anyone who needed it. Like this squog.

"I'll try," I said, sighing. "For the squog."

"Great." Doctor Frank clapped his hands together. "Now, lie back, shut your eyes, and listen to my voice."

I lay back in the molded chair he had set up parallel to the squog's flat table. The overhead lights hurt my eyes, and I squinted. Doctor Frank raised the chair with a foot lever and began to attach some small devices – probably sensors – to my head and chest.

"You may hear me moving about," Doctor Frank said, "but just ignore me."

I shut my eyes. *Ignore him.* Ignore the painful breathing of the squog beside me and the smell of damp fur. Easy.

"Good. Now, quiet your mind. Stop the brain chatter. You want to relax your body. I'm sending you a little help. There. That should make you relax."

I felt a rush of something cool flow into me through the devices attached to my skin. It was such a pleasant change from the throbbing heat I'd felt for so long. I relaxed without trying.

"Your blood pressure is lowering; your heart rate is slowing. So is your breathing. Good. Yes. Do nothing, now. Let your mind be quiet."

I lay still, trying to do as he said.

"You may begin to hear a sound like waves, your hands and arms may grow numb, and you may feel as if you're floating. You should get a feeling of peace, of interconnection with other life. That's when you reach out to the energy of the squog. That's when you give the instructions to heal. Now. Heal the squog."

He made it sound simple. I reached out for the squog, feeling a little squeamish. Connecting to a squog was nothing like connecting to Elyle or Jonah.

Forget about Jonah, I thought. *He's gone. It's over.* Yet I couldn't block him from my mind. I wanted him back. I wanted to connect to him again.

"Stay relaxed," Doctor Frank warned.

Right. The squog. I reached out again. *Mur? Hello? Please, Mur?* It was as if my head was banging against solid stone. I couldn't break through. I wanted to help the squog, I really did. But without Mur, I was worse than useless.

I opened my eyes.

"I can't do it."

Doctor Frank sighed nosily. Then I noticed Rylant beside him, hands on hips and one eyebrow raised skeptically.

"What is she doing here?" I sat up, banging my head on an overhanging scanner. Doctor Frank must have lowered it while my eyes were closed.

Rylant raised both eyebrows.

Be careful with her, I reminded myself, rubbing my head. It was hard not to blame her for everything that had happened. If only she hadn't investigated me. If only she hadn't interrogated Dad, I mean Leonard. And Mother. If only she hadn't uncovered their secret.

"Why so angry?" Rylant asked in her raspy voice. "I'm only here to help."

That kind of help I didn't need. "I don't like being watched," I said.

"Hmm." Rylant frowned at me. "You know, Lenni, Purity is here to protect you. Don't you agree, Doctor Frank?"

Doctor Frank nodded dutifully.

Yeah, right, I thought. *Just like Purity protected Redge, Duke's brother, and Febber.*

Rylant continued. "Our mandate is to regulate and protect the gene pool – for you, for me, for everyone in the Purity settlements and beyond. We aren't out to hurt anyone. In fact, we work to heal natural constructs, and we only regulate unnatural constructs. We heal them, too – animal or human – whenever possible."

Sure you do, I thought.

Then Rylant pointed to the squog, who was now shaking with each breath. "That's why we limit gen-eng on humans. Because mistakes are too easy to make."

I agreed with her there, but I didn't admit it.

"So, you see, Purity is here to help you. We try to undo the damage. We repair rather than replace a cell. Like with you. You did nothing wrong. You were a victim. But we have to clean up your parents' mistakes, and learn as much as we can in the process."

"So I'm just an experiment to you, after all?"

"Of course not. But just think about it. What if the procedures we develop from your test results could save

172

lives? How many lives would it take until the sacrifice of one person would be acceptable? What if we could save the lives of one million people? Or countless future generations? Is the sacrifice of one worthwhile if it means we could save many?"

I didn't say anything. "So I should just sacrifice myself for Purity? Is this squog a sacrifice, too?"

"Not a sacrifice. It's more like a public service. Caring for your children and your children's children. That's why I'm going to request that you do whatever Doctor Frank says. It's simple. Your healing abilities could help countless people. I'm sure you'll agree."

Doctor Frank nodded, happy to agree with anything Rylant said.

"Oh, sure. I'm so glad to help," I said, pushing as much saccharine at her as I could.

She glanced at Doctor Frank, then back to me. Her jaw clenched. "I'm sure you are."

Doctor Frank rubbed nervously at the rash on his head, but I got some satisfaction at the way Rylant slammed the door on her way out.

downpour

Four days later, the rain was hammering Dawn, dripping down my window in long, snaky currents. I longed to feel the outside air on my skin, to inhale more than the sterile vapor of the medical unit, and I cursed Purity for keeping me from the wet earth smell that would follow the storm. Since June, the steady heat had withered most plants, other than lifewort. Now the winter rains would make the air chokingly humid then, finally, cool it.

I sighed, turning from the window to pace another loop around my insufferable burgundy room. I couldn't listen to one more online lecture or endure any more tests. Doctor Frank still wanted me to heal something, anything. He hoped that he could strengthen me, somehow make me regain my abilities. He wanted to isolate the offending genes and find a way to reprogram them. Would that make me unable to heal again or help me repeat it? I didn't care either way. I just kept hoping that my visit with Jonah had been a nightmare – that he might still walk through that door and hold me like he had before. It was a pathetic dream, and I hated myself for wanting it, especially because it made the return to reality as pleasant as shattering a glass jar over my head. If only I could have found comfort in sketching, but that, too, had been denied me.

When I could stand my room no longer, I wandered out into the hall, nodding to my annoyingly responsible Purity guard. This one was about ten years older than me, with slick black hair and chiseled cheekbones. The upward tilt of his chin gave him an arrogant air, and he looked at me as if I were going to infect him.

"Shall we go visit Redge?" I asked in a sarcastic, chilly tone.

Not waiting for his response, I turned sharply left, knowing he would be two steps behind me, straight-backed and superior.

Redge's room was in the same ward – the restricted quarters reserved for skidge. I knocked on his door, waited a minute, then ambled in, but the burgundy room, a mirror of my own, was empty. Then I remembered. It was Monday, so he would be at the Academy. He was still allowed to attend; in fact, Doctor Frank insisted on it. Not that I wanted to go. I wouldn't want to meet up with anyone I knew. Like Jonah, if he hadn't left for his new life yet. Or even worse, Jobey Mendleson and his marauding gang of genetically perfect thugs. Suddenly, I got this image in my head of being surrounded by Jobey and his cronies as they jabbed and prodded me, taunting endlessly, while Jonah watched without helping. It was so similar to my dream of fire that it made me pause. My whole family had known I was skidge, had watched me walk into this mess without a warning. Now, Jonah had deserted me. They'd all left me to burn.

I rambled back up the hall with a wild restless energy and nothing to do except mull over depressing thoughts. I still had two hours until my next test, which wasn't much to look forward to. I considered spitting on my untalkative companion, just to watch him writhe in infected DNA, but it wasn't worth the trouble I'd get into. Maybe he had to go through cleansing after every shift — that would be a satisfying punishment for his stuck-up smirk.

Then, as I rounded the corner to the medic station, I bumped into Redge with his own Purity guard, returning from the Academy.

"Hey, Len. Wow, did I have a day! I was at the artificial reality labs. Those things are pure! Jay Downs, the lab tech, boosted the sensory input into my legs. I was walking, if only in my mind!"

Redge was grinning and pushing his wheels with gusto. So much for hating the Academy. Even his Purity guard couldn't dampen his spirits.

"Great," I said, trying to sound enthusiastic.

Redge and I turned back to his room with our shadowy companions.

"Guess what else I did?" Redge lifted his front wheels off the floor then wiggled the back of his chair from side to side in a wheelie dance. I noticed his finger-tips were practically healed from that Blass game incident.

"What?" I asked, wondering where he'd found such enthusiasm.

"I told Doctor Frank that I would do it."

We entered Redge's room, leaving the guards behind.

"Do what?" I kicked the door shut, enjoying the loud thump.

"The procedure." Two round circles of pink colored Redge's cheeks. His lips curved into a smile that I rarely saw.

"Really?"

"He's going to do it tomorrow. It's all because of you."

"Me?"

"You said that if you were me, you'd let Doctor Frank try again. Remember? That's what started me thinking."

"Oh, well, I didn't understand then." Redge trying another procedure – that conversation had happened so long ago that I'd almost forgotten it.

"But you did."

"No, I didn't." I snapped at him, then wished I hadn't. "How could I? I used to think I was normal. Now I'm skidge. I only wish I knew who I was meant to be. What I was supposed to be like."

"Listen to yourself!" Redge said, his smile annoying now. "You haven't suddenly been turned into skidge. You always were. The difference is that now you make people uncomfortable."

"Don't remind me." When I first noticed Redge's wheelchair, I was repulsed. Now, others felt that way about me. Jonah did. I frowned, hating Redge's words.

"You're the same as you were before. The only change is in them." Redge motioned vaguely toward the hall. "They're the ones who don't get it. They believe whatever Purity tells them to believe."

"You sound like that guy Duke from the cafeteria," I said, which wasn't really a compliment. I had liked Rae, but Duke had been too wired.

"Yeah? Maybe I do. Maybe some of his ideas make sense to me."

"I can't make sense of anything right now." I turned to leave. I didn't want to bring Redge down when he was so excited, and I couldn't share in his excitement. Doctor Frank knew enough to create Redge, but from what I'd seen he wasn't much good at curing me, much less his own rash. "What time is your procedure?"

"Ten."

"I'll wish you luck at ten," I said, trying to sound hopeful, like I believed Doctor Frank could actually heal.

The walk back was too short and uneventful. Redge's cheerful talk had made me feel more miserable, and I sulked down the hall, glowering at the medics and my guard along the way. I arrived back at my room just as Rae was coming out.

"Rae! What are you doing here?" I asked, almost forgetting to mope.

I didn't want visitors who would treat me like a freak, but Rae was safe. She wouldn't make me feel any worse.

"Just dropping off some room service." Rae grinned and headed back into my room.

I followed, seeing a plastic glass of clear blue liquid on the table.

"Glacier Juice!" Rae had brought me a drink? Why would she do that? It was an unexpected comfort, but enough to make me half-smile.

Rae nodded. "I thought you'd appreciate a little company."

"Thanks." I sighed noisily then shut the door, blocking the guard's view of us, although I'm sure he was still listening.

Rae picked up my slate. "Mind if I play a little music?"

"Sure," I said, wondering why she'd want to.

Rae grinned at my bewildered expression. "Music's a good distraction from your troubles." She tapped the stylus on my slate until she'd selected a song. Soft classical violins began to play. "And it also makes eavesdropping more difficult."

I nodded. "I should have thought of that."

Rae shrugged. "Guess you were preoccupied. Now, have a drink. You did like it, didn't you?"

"Yeah, it was great." We sat side-by-side on the edge of my bed, listening to the flutes answering the violins. "Do you want some?" I asked, raising the glass to her.

"No, you go ahead. I can make one for myself any old time."

"I suppose you can," I said, my voice falling. Most people were free to go wherever they wanted, to do whatever they wanted, except me.

"Now, don't get too down," Rae said. "You're not alone in this."

"I don't know about that." I snorted, then took a sip. The drink was the same cool explosion of sweet then sour. I took a long swallow then noticed Rae's twisted hand in her lap. Funny how it didn't seem strange to me anymore.

"There are others in your same predicament right now," Rae continued.

"Other skidge besides Redge?" The idea sickened me – more people hiding out or being persecuted by Purity. "Where?" I hadn't seen others on this floor. "Duke said that, but I wasn't sure if I believed him."

"Well, some will be hiding," Rae began slowly, thoughtfully, her voice softer than the music. "And there's Jay and Vishna. You remember the folks that Duke was talking to that day we met?"

He had been ranting, not talking. "The ones in the wheelchairs?"

"Uh-huh. They're both caught up in Purity's net, too, staying here at the unit."

"Were they just discovered, too?" I took another sip, letting the icy juice glide down my throat. The chill spread through me, cooling my skin and stilling my ever-dizzy head. Rae's drinks were better medicine than anything Doctor Frank could muster. Or maybe I just enjoyed her company.

"No, they were staying over at Detention Block, but they've come here for some medical work. Jay's a clone, made for parts, and he's aging too rapidly. Vishna is being fitted for a new leg, since Purity didn't like the look of hers."

"What are people thinking?" I exploded. I'd heard too many horror stories about skidge, and suddenly anger at Purity welled up in place of my despair. "How can they do this to other living beings? It's terrible."

It seemed no one was ethical or kind anymore. Even Jonah had abandoned me when I needed him, betrayed me for a career with Purity. And for the first time, I began to hate Jonah for what he'd done. If that was how he played, then I was glad I'd found out about it now.

Rae glanced furtively toward the hall then turned the music up. It had reached a crescendo of drums and violins.

"There are people enough to give them a hand." Rae continued. "And they don't have to stay in Dawn. There's always the Beyond."

I shuddered. "Send them to the Beyond! That's worse than Purity."

Rae chuckled. "You've been listening to too much Purity propaganda. The Beyond isn't so bad."

"Yeah?" I didn't know whether to believe her. I'd only ever heard about misbegotten skidge attacking people, power outages that lasted for months, and other tales of chaos.

"The Beyond has got some harsh folk, just like here, but mostly it's full of people like you, struggling to make a life in this world." Rae was drumming my stylus against her leg in time to the music. "I lived in the Beyond for over fifteen years. I only applied to come to Dawn to help out folks like you, Jay, and Vishna. Purity let me in, so I guess I serve some purpose. I just try to offer what comforts I can." She pointed to my drink.

Maybe it was the drink, or maybe it was Rae's friendly face. Either way, it was easy to listen to the reassurances of this woman I barely knew, even though I was sure Rylant would try to make me miserable again, as soon as possible.

I tipped my glass to Rae. "You make me feel like I can survive this whole experience, somehow."

"You can." Rae nodded. "And you have more help than you realize."

not my father

The next morning I was up early for a battery of tests. I lumbered back a few hours later, still groggy and resenting Doctor Frank and Rylant more than ever. They had been pumping different drugs into me to try to induce a theta state, but I'd only become bleary-eyed and disorientated, making their ridiculous dreams of healing even more impossible.

No more tests, I vowed silently, grating my teeth as every step jarred my throbbing head. *No matter what Rylant threatens.*

Back at my burgundy purgatory, I threw one last glare at my Purity guard and stumbled toward bed to sleep it off, only to find Leonard lying there. His large shoes, made from lifewort plastic, had left winter mud on my blanket. One arm covered his face.

"Dad?" The word flew from my lips before I could remind myself that he was no longer my father.

He jumped then squinted at me.

I wasn't ready to see him. He'd caught me off guard. Well, he'd never have forgiveness from me.

"Lenni!" He looked better than he had during the Purity interrogations, but not by much. He had more color in his cheeks and he had shaved. He sat up with a wobble, then came over to me. "Let me see you."

Holding me by the shoulders, he examined my face and ran his hands lightly up and down my arms, raising goosebumps. He stared curiously, just like Jonah had.

I stiffened, hoping everyone wouldn't examine me that way. Leonard wrapped his arms around me. He smelled like the outdoors, like refreshing rain.

"I'm glad to hear you call me Dad."

I pulled free, took a few steps back, and folded my arms across my chest as a barrier. Desperate to lie down, I forced myself to resist any of his attempts to reconcile. This was no simple betrayal. Words couldn't repair what he'd done.

"What are you doing here, Leonard?" I kept my voice steady.

"Leonard, huh?" He sighed and sat on the edge of my bed. "I can't blame you for being angry." He ran his fingers over his head. "But I'm here because I care about you. That must count for something."

I was silent. What he did, choosing who I would be, wasn't his decision to make. He shouldn't have interfered with who I was supposed to be.

"Come on, Lenni. Maybe if you let me explain."

"I saw your interrogation. You don't need to explain."

"They showed you that?" He sounded as if it were inappropriate viewing. Well, what did he think I'd been through?

I nodded, and my head spun. I needed to sit down, but I wasn't going to sit on the bed with him.

Leonard wiped his eyes. He examined one shoe in detail.

"I thought you were in Detention." My voice was hard.

"They released me. I'm heading the clean-up operation for lifewort." His face brightened and he almost smiled. "GrowTech is about to become an agent for genetic purity. Ironic, isn't it?"

"You would work for them?" I couldn't believe it. "Who?"

"Purity."

"Why not? I'm thinking of creating plastic-eating bacteria to destroy the plants. Then I could redesign lifewort from the ground up. Or maybe a supervirus to attack and alter the plant's DNA. Either way, I . . ."

"You just don't get it, do you? You don't think you did anything wrong. You don't even think you need to apologize."

"Apologize? For cleaning up lifewort?"

"For making me skidge!"

"No, Lenni." He shook his head, obviously rattled. "You're not skidge. You're special, unique. We gave you everything – the best we could offer. And you can do things that no one else can. Even more than I expected. I heard you healed Elyle. That's amazing! You should be proud of who you are."

I almost laughed out loud. "I think *you've* got it wrong. I'm not special and I'm not amazing. I'm skidge. A sub-human specimen. You can't change that." My voice was icy. He didn't begin to understand how he'd hurt me. He thought that making me skidge was doing me a favor.

"Don't talk like that. We can get you through this. You have some health problems, but my people can do some tests and regulate your condition. We'll talk to Purity and work this whole thing out. You'll see."

"I'm not lifeweed, Leonard. I'm not some plant that you can clean up."

"Lifewort," Leonard corrected, his voice rising. "Why does everyone always call it lifeweed?" His shoulders slumped, and I regretted my mistake. I admired lifewort. Why had I said that? Just to hurt him. Or *did* I think of lifewort as a weed now? If it really was destroying ecosystems, I suppose it should be stopped.

"I'm sorry. Lifewort," I muttered.

"It's all right." He sighed. "I deserved it. And lifewort has caused a mess. I guess I've made some mistakes. You must be furious with me."

The bed creaked as he stood. He went to the window and stared out.

I took the chance to collapse onto my bed. Maybe he did understand. I rolled onto my side toward Leonard and tucked the pillow under my head, grateful for its support.

Leonard didn't speak for a long time. He just examined the cloud-covered sky as if it could give him answers. I thought he might leave. Then he said without turning around, "Hubert and his anti-genetics association filed against GrowTech. I'm not surprised. First, Purity finds out about you, then the lawsuit. But, your mother . . ." He wiped his eyes again. "She took the most precious thing from me – my daughter."

Poor Leonard. So he knew how Mother had used another man's DNA instead of his. He was Mother's victim, too. "When did you find out what Mother did?"

"Purity had to tell me." He turned, sighing so deeply that his chest shuddered. "It's hard to imagine that your mother was once the sensitive girl I first met."

"Mother – a sensitive girl?" I couldn't imagine that.

"Of course she was sensitive. She was always worried about you – always working to prevent others from finding out." He paused. "But know this, Lenni. You're still my daughter. DNA patterns don't build a relationship. I've put so much into you that you're mine, no matter what the tests show. Here, look at this."

He pulled an image up on his slate then passed it to me. The title read "Projection of Hannix Child at Age 15." It was an image of me. Of what I had been programmed to look like. It could have been taken last month.

The picture slammed it home for me – Leonard and Mother had sat around considering what kind of child they wanted then made sure it happened. All thoughts of forgiveness vanished. He would never understand what he'd done – controlling me, molding me, constructing me. He was proud of it.

I opened my mouth to tell him off when Elyle walked in. She looked from me to Leonard. The air was stretched tight between us.

"Elyle!" I said, surprised to see her.

"I'll come back later." Elyle turned to leave.

"No, stay," I said. If anything, the picture proved that it was too late to talk to Leonard. He would never understand.

Elyle looked questioningly at Leonard. He nodded. She shut the door and leaned against it. It must have still been somewhat warm outside because she was wearing a light shirt and skirt. Her cheeks were pink and her eyes bright. I was glad to see her healthy, if a little tired. I still felt responsible for her.

"I just stopped in to see Redge, but he wasn't there," Elyle said. "I wanted to give you two time to talk."

"Redge is in surgery. Doctor Frank is trying to fix his legs again."

"Really?" One of Elyle's eyebrows rose into a peak.

"Yes."

"Did you see what I left you?" Elyle pointed behind me.

"What?"

I twisted on the bed and saw a small cloth bag on the side table. The cloth had a red and blue paisley pattern.

"What is it?" I sat up. My head had cleared slightly.

"Open it later, once we've gone," Elyle suggested.

"Do I have to wait?"

Elyle glanced at Leonard and shrugged. "It's private, but it's up to you."

Then I knew what it was: my waterstone. I didn't care if Leonard saw it. I wanted to open it now. I unknotted the tasseled cord that bound the bag. The waterstone was heavy in my hand.

"It's my waterstone! You got it back for me!" I'd keep it with me always now.

The gray and white flecked stone was cool, soothing. I stroked it, admiring it from all angles, remembering how Elyle had promised it would protect me. Well, it hadn't, but she had tried. And it was still beautiful and intriguing.

"What is it?" Leonard peered at it.

Even though Elyle had said the waterstone was private, I had to explain. "Elyle made it for me. It's a waterstone." I beamed at Elyle.

"Oh."

I ran my fingers over the raised image of the woman — her head, shoulders, arms, and body. It reminded me of drawing, how Elyle and I had once both been artists. I longed to sketch again, to feel the pleasure of it. Looking at the waterstone gave me a yearning, an aching desire for the past.

"What do you see?" Elyle asked.

I moved my head from one side to another, examining it. "Well, before, I thought it was a woman reaching out for something." I paused. "Now, I don't. She's pulling something toward herself, something that I can't see."

"Hmm, yes." Elyle placed an arm over my shoulder and we gazed at the waterstone together. "Maybe."

"Thanks." I stood to hug Elyle tightly. She smelled of lavender again, and I breathed it in deeply. After days and days of my world being slowly torn apart, Elyle had brought me a moment of happiness.

"I crafted the stone to help you, Lenni," Elyle began in her calm way, once we'd pulled apart. "I always hoped you wouldn't need it – that Purity would never find out about you." She stroked my hair. "I expected that you'd find out some day, but I'd hoped it wouldn't be like this. I wanted so desperately to protect you from those who might seek to injure you, and to help you discover who you are, what you're meant to do."

I looked intently at her. She spoke with such conviction, sure that the stone could do all that. I had needed protection over the last while. In fact, everything had gone horribly wrong just after I came to the unit, after my waterstone had been taken from me. Maybe it did have power, just like my sketches had. Or maybe I just had to believe it had power so I could hope.

"How are you, Lenni?" Elyle asked, softly.

I sighed, and paced the room, ignoring Leonard. "I don't know. They keep doing tests, and this fever never leaves me. I feel like it's a punishment. I have to study, but I don't care much about it. And I can't even sketch because I've lost Mur." I didn't care if Leonard heard about Mur. I couldn't pass up this chance to talk to Elyle. She was the only one who could understand. I held back a sob. "Oh, Elyle, I just wish it were a nightmare that would end, but it goes on and on."

Leonard glanced unhappily at me, then away.

"Stay strong, Lenni. Like a rock." Elyle leaned close to me and whispered, "Remember that all they did was give the initial recipe a boost. You did the rest."

"Maybe." I smiled.

"Now, I have something special planned for us." Elyle's tone changed to be more serious, less whimsical. "You may not be pleased, but I think it's important."

"What is it, Elyle?"

"Mara's been transferred here for some medical attention. She's down on the third floor, and I've arranged for a visit. We need to talk."

"No." How could Elyle even suggest it? I glanced at Leonard. Surely, he wouldn't want to see her?

"I know you're angry and hurt, Lenni," Elyle spoke in her soothing voice, "but we've got to work this through. You can't ignore your mother, and Leonard has already agreed to it, for your sake. It'll be best for everyone if we sit down together. Don't you want to understand how all this happened?"

"Why should I? She's done enough. I have nothing more to say to her."

"Then do it for me. I think you'll want to hear what we have to say."

family reunion

How did I let Elyle talk me into this? I thought, as the elevator doors opened onto a waiting area and a large medic station. This floor was busier than mine, filled with people waiting for boosts or other ordinary treatments. People who managed to survive under the shadow of Purity. It was a world from long ago, a world I didn't fit into anymore, a world I'd been expelled from. I held back as Elyle and Leonard led the way out of the elevator. Flanked by a Purity guard on each side, we lined the back wall of the elevator like statues. You'd think I'd be able to get some regular clothes to wear to the normal-people floor.

"Mara has changed," Elyle was saying. Then she noticed I wasn't following her. "What are you doing?"

Leonard turned, too, puzzled.

"Come on." The guard on the left nudged me with his elbow. I supposed that touching me through the cloth of his uniform wasn't too infectious.

I hesitated. Through the open door, I could see a mother with short blonde hair bending over a young girl, who was crying desperately. The girl was cradling her arm and rocking back and forth, obviously in pain. Poor kid. It was probably just a broken arm, so easy to fix, yet enough to hurt. These were simple people, who might be hassled by Purity but not hounded by them. I envied them, but they looked harmless enough.

Then the elevator door began to slide shut, and the guard on the right slammed a button to hold it open. "That's enough. Get going." He didn't dare to touch me, but his words were hard enough that I knew I had to move or get sent back up to my room.

Get it over with, I told myself. I was only going to see Mother because of Elyle, and right now it hardly seemed worth it.

I stepped out, keeping my eyes on the floor. The guards edged closer, blocking me from the two rows of people on either side, waiting in red plastic chairs. Like I was going to make a break for it, or reach out and contaminate an innocent bystander.

We were halfway down the aisle of chairs when I heard a kid squeal beside me.

"Momm-mmeee!" wailed the fragile voice. "It's the girl from the news!"

There were gasps around me. Someone dropped a slate. The crash ricocheted off the walls. The guards pressed closer.

My face grew hot and my head pounded. The girl from the news. That was me. A monster shown on the *New North Report*. Beware. Skidge are among us.

Hunting us down. What horrible things had they said about me?

I dared to raise my head. The young girl with the broken arm stood facing me. Her mother was gripping her shirt, her hands clenched. The girl's chin trembled. White-blonde hair hung over her huge eyes, which were wide with terror.

People began to mutter.

"What is she doing here?"

"This is hardly the place for skidge!"

"There are children here!"

I had to endure this to see Mother?

When the guard nudged me forward, I stumbled on, their words ringing in my head. What had I become? A beast in a Purity advertisement. A warning. An example. Purity had probably told them that I had infected Elyle, rather than healing her.

I made it down the hall somehow, lost in the sting of the moment, following the slump of Leonard's shoulders as we edged closer to Mother.

Elyle stopped us outside a closed door, secured by a single Purity guard. Her sympathetic eyes landed on me. "I'm sorry, Lenni. I never thought . . ."

The guards nodded to each other then stood at ease, ignoring us.

I shrugged. This would happen everywhere I went, over and over again. I would never be welcome anywhere, by anyone. I glanced at Leonard. He was looking miserably away from me, glumly examining the door handle.

"Well, I just wanted to warn you about Mara before we go in." Elyle sighed. "You'll find her much worse."

I exhaled noisily. Leonard rubbed his eyes. I would never be ready for this. My head was still clouded with the drugs Doctor Frank had injected, my skin was clammy, and my stomach churned.

Elyle opened the door. Leonard and I followed her into a large, light-filled room, much bigger than mine. A bouquet of flowers scented the air. The walls were a warm yellow. The window overlooked Center Block and the throng of people scuttling about the square. The change of view was so refreshing that I envied Mother her room. Then I looked toward the bed.

Pillows supported the figure among the blankets. Without her glasses, Mother's face appeared rounder, more pasty. Her pale blue hospital gown was brighter than her cheeks. With her eyes closed and her arms limp on the covers, I was startled by her frailty. This was not the powerful, controlling Mother I knew.

"Mara," Elyle whispered. She lifted Mother's wilted hand, holding it gently.

A food tray lay untouched on the side table, and the scent of spiced meat turned my stomach. *Don't wake up,* I thought. *I don't want to do this.*

Mother's eyes fluttered open, glazed with sleep. She glanced around but didn't seem to recognize any of us.

"Mara, can you hear me?" Elyle whispered. "Leonard and Lenni are here. Do you remember what we talked about?"

"Elyle? Don't leave me again."

Still giving orders. Mother rubbed her head, tangling her knotted hair even more. She shifted higher on the pillows and blinked then squinted at me.

"You!" Her voice wavered but the tone was accusing.

Familiar anger welled up in me. "What?"

"You had to show off. You had to heal Elyle. If only you'd been quiet."

"Now, Mara," Elyle began.

"I'm not talking to her," I backed away. "I don't need this."

"I told you to be careful," Mother continued in a whining voice, "but you had to make friends with boys and sketch strangers in the commons. You had to lead Purity right to us!"

"Don't talk to me!" I shook with anger, hating Mother, hating this pattern of accusations, hating Leonard and Elyle for allowing it to continue.

Elyle gave Leonard a pleading look.

"Please, Mara." Leonard tried to pat her arm. "Quiet down. This isn't Lenni's fault. She didn't know."

Mother's dazed look vanished and she concentrated her gaze with clear, angry eyes. "You did this to us!"

"I never . . ." I couldn't utter the words.

"Enough Mara!" Leonard's voice rang out. His eyes were fiercer than I'd ever seen them. "This is not Lenni's fault. It's ours." His voice fell. "All our fault."

I couldn't believe my ears. Leonard was standing up for me.

"You?" Mother turned her narrowed focus to Leonard. It was as if she could only concentrate on one person at a time, and it took a great effort.

"Yes, Mara. It's Leonard. And it's time we squared things with Lenni."

After all these years of letting Mother run our lives, Leonard was helping me.

"You have no claim here." Mother half-rose off her pillow. "You're not her father."

Leonard's face paled. "You just try to take her from me," he hissed.

Mother sunk back, startled.

I glanced at Elyle, who was looking from Leonard to Mother, amazed. "This isn't what we talked about. Remember, we're here for Lenni," she begged. "To explain."

Leonard nodded, still looking fierce. "That's right, Elyle. We're here for Lenni," he said, but he didn't take his eyes off Mother.

"Leonard." I was struck by his strength, his willingness to finally defend me. "Dad." I touched his shoulder, saying the word deliberately – maybe to spite Mother, or maybe because I meant it. I wasn't sure yet, but it felt right to say it.

He finally, reluctantly, pulled his eyes off Mother, and gave me a grateful smile. Then he sighed, shuddering deeply. "I tried to tell you before, Lenni, but all my words came out wrong. We never meant to get you into this mess. We just wanted to help you to be all you could be. If only you could understand all we've done. I had to falsify your DNA records, and every time you went for a medical checkup, I bribed the doctor. And the worry!" He wiped his forehead. "We were always concerned, always watching out for you." He glanced at Mother. "I'm not sure we realized the toll this would take on all of us – the great effort we would have to put into protecting you."

They'd done all that? "But why use gen-eng in the first place?"

"To give you every benefit we could!" Leonard threw up his hands. "I know you can never understand. I know you'll probably never forgive me. But we did everything for you. Even the mistakes."

"Your mistakes!" Mother piped up. "Not mine." She smiled smugly. "I knew what I was doing."

"Now, Mara," Elyle said. "You promised to talk to Lenni. Tell her now. Go on."

Mother stopped, confused. She seemed more dependent on Elyle. "Tell her?" She paused. "Yes." She ignored Leonard and centered on me.

I stared her down, guarded against the next attack, the next insult.

"It's wasn't easy, but I did it," she began. "Leonard's mother died a terrible death from cancer, and I had to protect you from that fate. So I did a little research of my own," she smiled proudly, "and came up with the perfect specimen. It was a challenge, yes, but it was worth it. His name was Ricard Brahan."

"Brahan?" I glanced at Elyle. The same last name!

"Yes, Lenni." Elyle nodded.

"Elyle, what is she saying?" Leonard demanded.

So he didn't know who my real father was either.

"Lenni's biological father was my husband," Elyle admitted, her face solemn.

The room was silent, except for the buzz of energy between us. Leonard – poised, tense, so furious at this news that he seemed ready to strike someone down. Mother – smug and plump on her mountain of pillows.

Me – so astounded that I could have fallen over. And Elyle – a bridge between us all.

"I knew nothing until after he died," Elyle began, "when the notice came from the DNA bank. It seems he'd donated just before his accident. I never understood why. Maybe he'd wanted to help people who couldn't have children – donate so they could conceive. The ironic thing is that we'd been planning our own family." Elyle's voice quavered. "I followed it up because I was grieving. It was my only link to him. You can't imagine how much I wanted him back."

It explained so much. Why I wasn't like my parents. Why I felt so different from them. And Elyle, I wasn't related to her by blood, but she was my mother, in a way. My stepmother.

"So Ricard," I tried out his name – the name of my father, "he designed the waterstone basin. He was an artist, too?"

"When I found you, I wanted to care for you, to help you as much as I could. I looked for signs of Ricard in you, and found them everywhere. And the waterstone, his craft – it was important for me to share that with you, to shape a stone as he would have done."

"Why didn't you tell me?"

"It wouldn't have made you any safer." Elyle shook her head sadly.

The door suddenly burst open and Rylant exploded into the room. "I think we have all the information we need." She sounded triumphant.

"Not you!" Mother began.

Rylant put a hand on Elyle's arm and started directing her to the door.

"No!" Mother was rising off the bed, putting a shaky foot on the floor.

"Do you see now, Lenni?" Elyle pleaded over her shoulder, as if she'd expected Rylant's interruption. "We did everything for you. All of us. Even Ricard."

"Time for a little questioning." Rylant nodded at the three guards who had entered Mother's hospital room.

"Don't take her!" Mother began to sob pathetically.

Dazed and angry, Leonard stared at Elyle, then at Mother, who was stumbling across the floor after Elyle. I wanted her to stay, too – to ask her more questions, to understand what was happening. But I also understood that Elyle had sacrificed for me, revealed this information even though Rylant had been listening because she knew I needed to hear it, to possess the whole truth, to make sense of it.

Rylant swept Elyle from the room, as Elyle called, "Find your peace, Lenni! It's all I ever wanted for you."

I nodded to Elyle, not trusting my voice to speak. It was so much to absorb, to process at once. My knees felt weak. My body shook with longing to rescue my stepmother. "Leave her alone," I yelled at Rylant, but it didn't help.

"Bring her back!" Mother stumbled a few more steps, her chunky legs exposed below her robe.

The door thumped shut.

Mother sagged. She turned to me. "I can't do it," she moaned. "Not without Elyle."

We were the same — both wanting Elyle — and I hated it. I was about to twist away from Mother when her face blanched white then green. Her legs quivered. She wiped a shaky hand over her eyes then swooned, falling to the floor with a thud before anyone could catch her.

into the ache

I looked at Leonard, and our eyes locked. We'd seen Mother faint before. Now she'd betrayed us, and I suppose we both hated her for it. Yet a silent understanding passed between us then, and we became chillingly practical. No matter how much we despised her at that moment, we would help her.

"I'll get a medic," Leonard said, his voice strangely calm.

I nodded. "I'll watch her." I couldn't possibly lift her back onto the bed, and who knew what the medics would want to do with her.

Leonard made for the door. "And Lenni?" His look was frenzied, but his voice was composed. "I'm sorry."

"I know, Dad." My head still reeled from Elyle's news. I had two fathers now and two mothers. Life was more complicated than ever, but I was suddenly tired of fighting, tired of trying to understand everyone's complex motives. Forgiving Leonard had become easy, but Mother was different.

Then I was alone with Mother. Unable to leave because of the guards in the hall. Locked in with the woman who had done the most to hurt me, and the most to protect me. Had her illness been partly my fault? She'd only been trying to shield me. I found myself stroking my waterstone for comfort, and wondering if Mother, too, was a victim. She'd suffered years of worry and anxiety.

I examined Mother from a distance. She lay still on the hard floor, her eyes closed, her lips soft and open. It was such a different face from moments before. She looked depleted.

"Mother?"

I kneeled to watch her chest rising and falling slowly. Still breathing. When would the medics come? There had been a long line of people waiting for attention. Maybe they were too busy.

I didn't really want her to wake, didn't want to deal with her anymore. She would never be strong, and I would always be plagued by the effects of her poor health. Maybe the way to be finally free of her – to free us both – was to heal her. But I couldn't heal anymore. Could I? I closed my eyes.

Mur, are you there?

I waited for a response. Maybe Mur would come. Silence.

Mur?

I was foolish to try. I remembered how I had sketched Elyle and the others, but I didn't even have a slate. Could I do without? I began to trace an outline in the air above Mother.

An ache grew in my stomach, an ache for the loss of Mur and sketching, for Jonah's treachery, for Mother's scheming ways. A tangle of emotion lay embedded in my gut, as if all the pressure and stress had found harbor there. Although I tried again and again to connect with Mother, each time was a disappointment, just like with the squog. Finally, I dropped my hand and hung my head. I'd failed. I'd lost Mur. Once I'd been able to sketch and to heal, but the seizures and the fever had stopped all that. I'd overloaded myself. My art was lost to me forever.

I slumped beside Mother on the cold, sterile floor.

The ache inside me grew stronger. I curled over into a ball, trying to ease it.

Seizures, aches, fever. I could never trust my body again. I would never be what I had been. The ache tightened my chest now, like a band squeezing me.

I entered the growing ache. I had no choice. It was overpowering. The heat of it, the cramping. As if I were confined in chains, my muscles contracted, another seizure struggling to begin, straining against the device in my neck. I tried not to fear it, or question it. Just surrender to it. This ache, this failure and confusion, was all that was left.

Inside the pain, I somehow found myself thinking about how my body carried my history – my genetic code – who I was and who I had become. Every seizure. Every damaged cell. Every change Mother and Dad had made to me. Just like my genetic records, my body held it all: my birth, the joys and horrors of my lifetime, the passage of my ancestors, the father I would never know, the very flow of my life.

My body had taught me how to draw, how to heal, how to find Mur. Now it was teaching me to listen to the shifting current within – the pain and the subtle changes in temperature, muscles, tension, mood. Like currents reveal the movements of water, maybe my body would show me how to heal again.

I sunk further into the pain, letting it overwhelm me. I coiled around it, then stretched out long until the hurting was no longer my enemy. Gradually, it began to empower me, like Mur used to do. I was strong, directed. I reached out for Mother again, with hope as my guide and pain as my strength.

Then, Mother was before me, without Mur's help. Mother's energy body. I pushed my way inside. Her defenses were like a fortress of stone, but I'd learned to worm past.

Mother lay sleeping, her head resting to one side and one arm thrown up over her eyes as if shutting them was not enough. She was not terribly injured. A dark energy hugged her head, but it was graying already, without my help. Mother would recover from this latest fainting spell.

Then I noticed a woman in long silver robes standing at Mother's feet. Mur! Those fathomless eyes! The silver glow of her hair! My heart twisted in horror. How could Mur be with Mother?

I stood at Mother's head, facing Mur. Mur hadn't come back to me. She was here with Mother. How could she betray me, too! I stared from Mur to Mother and found my arms raised, ready to strike down a blow on Mother. I could crush her. Take back Mur. I had the strength.

No. I glanced at Mur's face, examining me now with cool observation. That was not the way.

I froze, stiff, and thought of my waterstone. What had Elyle said? It could guide me to myself? Then, like a flash of lightning, understanding came. The stone hadn't shown a girl reaching out. Her arms were offering a gift.

Give Mur to Mother? I couldn't. A swath of memories unfurled. My first moments with Mur. Mur guiding me to the commons to discover intuitive drawing. Mur piloting me toward Jonah. Giving Mur to Mother would be almost impossible.

But I had to. Saving Mother would liberate us both. I lowered my arms, stretching them wide, my hands open. I bowed to her sleeping form.

You can have Mur, Mother.

I opened my eyes to Mother's hospital room. My head was spinning, and lights flashed and twinkled on the edge of my vision. Not another seizure!

Mother sat up, shook her head, and looked about.

"Who's there? Lenni? Did you hear that voice? Where am I?"

I didn't know if I could forgive Mother for all the things she'd done. But I could show her that I wasn't going to fight for control. If Mur was with her, she would stay there. Maybe she was there for a reason. I began to sob great heaves. Mother had Mur now. Oh, how I missed her.

"Good-bye, Mur," I whispered.

"What are you crying for?" Mother sounded concerned.

The anti-seizure device in my head began to throb. I rubbed my fingers over it. It was warm. My skin had puffed out around it.

I became powerfully hot, as if a roar of fire had flamed up around me, as if my fever had intensified to unimaginable proportions, the heat of it licking my skin. The ground beneath me began to rumble. Cracks opened and traveled along my skin like snakes. Tiny cracks widening into crevices, threatening to break me apart.

Then the waves of heat slowly subsided. I became aware of Mother, sitting beside me on the floor, feet splayed, rubbing her eyes as if she'd just woken from a long, refreshing sleep. My skin was cooling; my body recovering its strength. I stared at my weak, still-trembling hands. I had reached out to Mother, and I had connected with her. Without Mur. It was an empty victory.

"Lenni? You all right?" I heard Dad's voice.

I pulled my eyes from my hands and saw Dad with a cluster of medics gathering around. *Was Mur in each one of them,* I wondered, *or just in Mother?*

I stood up. My pulsing fever, my aching muscles were fading. "I'm fine."

Could Mur have been only in my mind — a subconscious dream to guide me through my days? But no, Mur had been too real. She'd shown me the vast distances beyond my small existence. I'd known the joy of sketching with her, the emptiness of being only one, and, now, the bittersweet certainty that I was whole without her.

Or was I without her? I was full, complete, stronger than before. Perhaps she was still with me, just in another way. Perhaps she'd always been there, even when I'd thought she hadn't been. Perhaps the trick was learning to make decisions without her — to guide myself in faith with her.

classified

Mother was fully cured; the medics confirmed it. She sat up brightly and chatted while they examined her. They reported to Dad that her heart rate had slowed and her muscles relaxed. They said the chemical change in her brain was a result of drug therapy that morning. Dad stared at Mother's healthy glow, at her attempts to apologize for deceiving us. It was bizarre, surreal, something out of a childhood dream. The only person missing from this happy family picture was Elyle.

I hoped Rylant would release her soon. She just couldn't hold Elyle, I told myself. Because Elyle had nothing to do with it. She hadn't even known Mother then. Yet Purity didn't play fair, and I knew I'd worry until I saw Elyle again.

The trip back to my floor was a blur. I marveled at the newness of the world, at the feeling of strength within me again. I knew that, with the twist of a thought, I could heal others. I could see into them with only a glance, turn up the dial to hear their subconscious. Their voices crowded into my mind, competing to be heard.

In my room, I devoured my lunch with a hunger I hadn't felt in weeks and pondered what had happened. I thought about the device in my neck – it had probably saved me from another seizure. And I thought about Mur – how I would never hear her voice again, feel the swirl of her breath through me, or look into her fathomless dark eyes. But I refused to mourn Mur. She wasn't gone; I had changed. I didn't need her in the same way anymore.

I played with my slate, making sketch after sketch, enjoying the pleasure of drawing again, until I felt refreshed. Yet I was careful to draw only objects or myself. Drawing other people could change them, and I'd learned from healing Elyle that it was not a power to use lightly. Professor Fwatt had said that an artist should be free to paint any subject matter, but art as healing was different. In a way, I'd lost my carefree days of art for the sheer joy of portraying the world around me. Now, my art had more serious consequences. If I went around healing anyone I wanted, wouldn't I be the same as my parents, creating people as I wanted them to be? Or was I just helping out people who were ill, like Doctor Frank did?

Then I remembered Redge. His procedure had been that morning. Maybe Doctor Frank had found a way to fix his legs. I hoped so, because then I wouldn't have to debate whether it was right or wrong for me to heal him.

My guard in the hall was new – a woman this time, with sharp eyes and pursed lips.

"I'm going to visit my friend," I told her, turning toward Redge's room.

She stepped in front of me. "I have no authorization for that." Her eyes flashed and she had one hand on her slate, ready to signal other guards.

"What? I've visited him before." It was a harsh reminder. I was still a prisoner.

"Not on my shift." She shook her head.

"It's in the same ward!" It wasn't like I was asking to go to the cafeteria to see Rae.

It took several transmits, and many frustrating conversations, but finally I was allowed to go.

I fumed down the hall beside her, hating Rylant and Purity with a new vengeance. I had to get out of this place. I couldn't stand being captive, a criminal because of my parents' crimes. But where would I go? Everyone in Dawn would know I was skidge by now.

Boom-buda-buda. Boom-boom-boom. Redge had jacked the volume of his Blass game so loud that the bass thudded in my chest as I entered his room, leaving my prissy-faced guard in the hall.

"Ready, Dawg?" he yelled over the music.

Even though I doubted Doctor Frank's abilities, I'd still hoped to see Redge walking. But he was in his bed wearing a hospital robe, his chair abandoned in the corner and his fingers plugged into the game controls in his lap. Not a good sign.

"Ready," Dawg answered.

"Let's go 'til it hurts."

Redge didn't hear me come in or even see me until I stood near him, watching the Blass opening visuals side-by-side on Dawg's slate and Redge's game screen. The Blass logos twisted and turned like two dancing clones, then divided into jagged pieces and blasted apart.

"How did it go?" I asked, without much hope, when the opening music had died down.

"Oh, Len. You're just in time to watch me blow past level sixteen."

"You're doing level sixteen? What, are you crazy? You'll destroy your fingers." His fingers were still scarred from the last time he'd played.

"Shh. If you're going to stay, be quiet."

I almost left then, but I knew he was hurting. I tuned into him and saw swirls of pain like clouds of angry red vapor within him. He wasn't ready for help. I sat down in his wheelchair with a sigh and pulled it over to watch the game.

Twin puzzles began to form — one on Dawg's display panel and the other on the game slate that Redge held. Jagged pieces streamed in from the edges of the screens as the puzzles began to spin and wobble.

Redge lassoed a piece, then positioned it in his puzzle. After a while, I could see that Redge was forming a complex 3-D tree shape, while Dawg had chosen a simple diamond. I didn't know much about Blass, but I knew that more points were awarded for complex shapes and that the penalty for losing became worse with each level.

A few minutes later, the pieces were whirling in faster, and pink bombs were swirling in to blast gaps in the puzzles. I gripped the arms of Redge's chair.

"Your strategy is flawed. You are not likely to win this level," said Dawg, as Redge's tree began to show gaps.

"Never say never."

Redge squinted at the screen. He positioned a blue piece to take the hit of a pink bomb.

"Yes!"

The blue piece exploded, but his incomplete tree was safe. He maneuvered a few more pieces into place. His tree was still riddled with holes, as if a woodpecker army had attacked it.

Dawg easily completed his diamond. I held my breath as I watched Redge struggle. He managed to blow off three pink bombs in a row, awarding himself a slew of green molded pieces. He filled in his gaps and finished the tree.

"Pure! I am better than Blass today! Level sixteen! Yeah!"

I took in a long breath. "Your fingers could have been shredded."

"At least I can feel my hands."

He sucked at one of his fingers. His previous puncture wounds were almost healed and I wondered if they were tender.

"Does that mean . . . ?"

"That I can't feel my legs. Good guess." His voice was sarcastic, stinging.

"Look, I'm sorry that it didn't work, but you don't have to take it out on me."

Redge sighed. "You're right. Sorry."

"So what happened?"

"Nothing. Doctor Frank injected regenerative cells into my legs and nothing happened." He sighed again. "Last night I dreamed that I was climbing a rock face at the ridge – the one by the waterfall. My toes wedged into a crevice, sunlight in my eyes – I made it to the top. Then I woke up." He punched a fist into his thigh, under the blanket. "Doctor Frank says give it a few days. He says the nerves might kick in later."

"I don't know about that, but I do know what could help . . . ." I still wasn't sure if I should heal him, but I couldn't resist when he was so down, so wounded.

"No, Lenni. Don't," said Redge. "I can't think about trying anything else. Not right now."

"But, Redge, just listen to me. I've got to tell you . . . ."

"Stop." His voice echoed off the bare walls. "I can't." He shook his head, closing his eyes. His message was clear. He wanted to stumble around in his own despair. He couldn't hear me. Maybe he would be better off without my help anyway.

"Lenni! I thought I might find you here." Doctor Frank entered the room, looking worried. "We need to talk."

"Doc! Aren't you going to check my legs?" Redge's voice had a hard edge. "Wait. Let me update you on my condition." He slapped his legs again. "They don't work!"

"Redge, please. I told you that the effects might not be immediate. After a few procedures, we should begin to see some progress."

"No, we won't. I'm not having another procedure. Ever."

"We'll have time to talk about this later, Redge. I really have something quite serious to discuss with Lenni. If you will please . . . ."

"What is it?" I could tell that Doctor Frank was nervous because the rash on his head was raw in one spot from where he'd been scratching it.

"I'd like to talk where we can't be overheard," he lowered his voice to a whisper and glanced at Redge then at the speaker near the door, "but I'm afraid we haven't time."

Redge gave me a look. What was going on?

"Music," I said. "We need some music, Redge." Doctor Frank had admitted that people were listening.

"What?" Redge squinted at me, confused.

"So no one can hear," I whispered.

"Oh." Redge fumbled with his slate. Soon, an upbeat, jazzy tune began to play.

Doctor Frank leaned closer, continuing to whisper. "Yes. Good. Well. Uh, I'm not supposed to be telling you this, but . . . Purity has completed their evaluation of your test results. The changes made to your DNA cannot be reversed, Lenni. We couldn't effect a change on a genetic level."

I nodded. It was no surprise, really. I never had confidence in Doctor Frank's methods.

"Well, uh, Purity has determined that your genetic mutations would be passed onto future generations if you were to have children. If fact, Purity is concerned about what damage you could do to others if your healing powers returned."

Redge gasped. "No!"

A chill blew through me. "What does that mean?"

"Yes, well, Lenni. Your reproductive classification has been revoked. That means no reproduction of any kind. You've been reclassified as a restricted. Do you understand? Purity will sterilize you." He spoke with finality.

"No!" I leapt up, sending Redge's chair spinning against the wall.

"You will be registered and all your actions and your whereabouts will be monitored." Doctor Frank was still talking. "You'll likely live here until your symptoms are under control, then be transferred to Detention Block or a work camp."

Detention Block! Work camp! A monitor! My head spun. After recovering my strength, how could this happen?

"Lenni, you've got to escape!" Redge blurted.

"Keep your voice down!" Doctor Frank hushed Redge, but he didn't warn me against escaping.

I was numb. Escape to where? Anywhere. Just get out. I glanced frantically around the room, finally settling on the window. The afternoon sky was clouded now, and I wished desperately that I could vanish into the billowing haze.

I should leave. I had to. Yet I was leaving so much behind: Elyle, Dad, Redge, and even Mother.

"We've got to help her, Doc." Redge was wiggling over to the edge of his bed, motioning for me to roll his chair closer. "We've got to get her out of here."

Yes, get out. Redge could help me get out. Then a stab of guilt hit me. What about Redge? I had the power

216

to heal him! Escaping didn't help him, Elyle, or anyone else left behind. But what could I do? Purity was coming now, for me.

"I should get my slate." I said, positioning the chair for Redge, my hands shaking.

"No." Doctor Frank was firm. "Do nothing to arouse suspicion."

"Then you will help," Redge said.

Doctor Frank scratched at his rash. "I can't jeopardize my position here. I've got my experiments to think about, and you're set up nicely, Redge. You don't know how hard I've worked to do that. But, Lenni, I can give you the name of someone to smuggle you out of Dawn. And I can promise to look the other way while you arrange things."

"You know how to get out of Dawn and you never told me?" Redge's face grew red. "Why didn't you ever help me get out?"

"Redge, you were taken from me shortly after you were created, and, remember, I was in Detention, too. I never had a chance. Why do you think I'm working so hard to fix your legs and get you educated? I know I can help you walk. Maybe even get your reproduction classification changed. You've been sterilized, but there's always cloning. We can work on you, but, right now, I can save Lenni."

"Cloning is illegal, Doc!" Redge sputtered out his words.

The music droned on, but I wondered if it was enough to cover this heated exchange.

"Please, Redge. Calm down," I begged. "I need your help." I felt terrible, urging him to help me when I hadn't helped him. But I couldn't get off this floor without him.

Redge glared more fiercely, yet he was silent.

"Listen, Lenni." Doctor Frank glanced behind him. "You need to contact a woman named Rae Makio. She works in the lower cafeteria. I've been in touch with her. She'll help you relocate."

"Rae?" I said, amazed. Then I remembered how she'd said she helped out skidge like me. Had she been dropping clues then? Maybe that was why she'd brought me the room service.

"From the cafeteria?" Redge gave me a look.

"That's right. Now go, Lenni." Doctor Frank urged. "I couldn't save Redge when they came for him, but maybe I can save you." He scurried to the door. "I'm . . . I'm sorry I can't help more," he whispered.

"Thanks for warning me." I had no time, but I had to ask about Elyle. "Can I ask you a favor?"

"What is it?"

"Well, Rylant has taken Elyle for questioning." Doctor Frank raised his eyebrows. "It's a long story. Could you please watch out for her, if you can? I'm hoping Rylant doesn't hold her long."

I felt badly for not telling Doctor Frank about healing Mother; he'd been so desperate to see me heal again. But Rylant would be coming for me and I wasn't sure that I completely trusted Doctor Frank, even now.

"If she did nothing wrong, she'll be released within hours. But I'll watch for her. Good luck." He opened the door, then slipped into the hall and was gone.

Redge, still glowering, began to speak into his slate. "Dawg, we've got work to do. First, disengage my monitor. Then we'll send the guards on a short mission."

Five minutes later, I was strolling down the hall with Redge in his Academy uniform and me still in my gown, music ringing in my ears, trying to look as if we were going nowhere special.

Please let this work, I begged. My stomach clenched and fluttered.

"The guards are taken care of," Redge said. "Dawg has cut through computer security, and, of course, there is a rather timely emergency staff meeting. I'll get a transmit to Rae — tell her to meet you in the back courtyard. I've used the route before," he said with a satisfied smirk. "We'll get you out of here. Don't worry."

"Thanks." I chewed my lip and peered both ways down the hall. No one in sight.

We headed to the freight elevator that would take us down to the cafeteria. Redge checked in with Dawg through his slate, but my slate was still in my room. Not that I needed it, since I could heal without it, yet it felt wrong to leave it — and my sketches — behind.

At least I had my waterstone, which I'd brought with me to Redge's room. It was my only link to Elyle. It was hard to leave without seeing her. And to think of Mother back in Detention Block soon. I didn't wish that on anyone. I'd miss Dad, too, and Redge. It was difficult to leave them all, but it was more difficult to ignore the truth — that I would be a prisoner forever if I stayed. Doctor Frank had given me an opportunity, and I knew I had to go, no matter what.

We rounded the corner to the hallway with the freight elevator, my bare feet cold on the tiled floor. The hall was stark white; the ceiling lights shone a cool blue. How wonderful it would be to get outside, to feel my feet on the earth and smell the rain coming. Almost there. Down the elevator, out into the courtyard, then away.

"Dawg, is the elevator in place?"

Instead of Dawg's voice, I heard a deep, gravelly voice. "Did you really think that trick would work again?"

Rylant. I spun around. Rylant was walking steadily down the hall toward us.

"How did she . . . ?" Redge whispered.

"I don't know," I said, my heart hammering. "But we've got to find a way past her."

collision

Rylant came to a halt before us. A sickening wave of panic welled up from my stomach. Blood pounded in my throat, and roared in my ears. *I have to get out,* I kept thinking. But how? The elevator was too far away. Probably more guards were on the way. How to get free?

"After your last prank," Rylant looked down at Redge as if he were a cockroach to be crushed, "the computers were instructed to alert me when your monitor's signal disconnected." She was enjoying this victory, even gloating.

"You have no right." Redge spluttered. His hand was in his lap, shoving his slate down beside his legs out of sight, protecting Dawg.

"We've played this game before." Rylant smirked at Redge, her voice chilling. "You're going back to your room before I decide to revoke your privileges. Lenni is coming with me."

No way! My hands began to sweat. I was frantic to get away, yet my feet were frozen in place. I had nowhere to run.

"Leave her alone! You can't take her. It's not right." Redge began to shift his chair back and forth, as if he could bust past her and make a break for it, pulling me after him.

Then I realized — since Rylant was here, maybe Elyle had been freed. I found a way through my terror to speak. "Where's Elyle?" I asked her.

Rylant gave me a twisted smile, considering her answer. But before she could speak, a voice called from behind us. "What's going on?"

Redge and I turned to see Doctor Frank, hurrying down the hall. What was he doing here?

"An escape attempt." Rylant's voice was grim, yet triumphant.

"Oh!" Doctor Frank's right eye twitched. "Can I help?"

Rylant gave him a slow, appraising glance, as if she were evaluating his loyalties. "Not necessary, Doctor. I've got everything under control. I was just about to accompany Redge back to his room."

And take me to be sterilized! I had to get away. I glanced at Redge, who was clenching his jaw in frustration.

Rylant began to marshal us down the hall in front of her. Doctor Frank kept pace beside Rylant. I suppose he was trying to help us, but there was nothing he could do unless he had another secret plan.

At the first corner, we turned left, back toward our rooms. *No, I can't just obey*, I thought as we tramped closer and closer. Soon, I'd be shipped off to Detention. I couldn't let that happen. I had to take control. I spun around to face Rylant. Confused, Doctor Frank and Redge stopped, too. No one else was in the hall.

"I know you've reclassified me," I said bluntly. "But there's something you don't know."

"Keep walking." Rylant jerked her chin at me.

I ignored her, and Doctor Frank's nervous stare. He probably thought I was going to tell Rylant that he'd warned me. "I healed my Mother today. I can heal again."

Redge gasped.

"You . . . w-what?" Doctor Frank stammered.

"It's true." I turned to Redge. "I tried to tell you before."

"Then why are you telling them?" Redge said, his voice filled with venom. "They'll just use you, test you, until you wear out."

It was exactly what I was afraid of, but I had to risk it, to trust my abilities.

"If this is true, then you can heal the squog," Rylant said, her eyes narrowing. There was some eagerness in her face. She wanted this, although not as much as Doctor Frank did.

"I can do better than that," I said.

Rylant's lip trembled. "What do you mean?"

I had to heal more than the squog. I had to change Rylant. It was the only way to stop her from doing more unspeakable things to innocent people. No matter if I was just like Doctor Frank when he'd created Redge, or

Mother and Dad when they'd chosen me. Rylant was hurting too many, and I had to end it if I could.

I shut my eyes, letting my strength gather within me.

"What are you doing?" Rylant's voice was rough, demanding.

Harsh hands shook me. I kept my eyes closed and focused intensely on a tiny spot at the center of the vast space that was my mind, my existence, my soul. Rylant couldn't reach me there.

You can do this, I encouraged myself, just like Mur would have done.

"Stop that right now!" Rylant yelled close to my face. Maybe she'd guessed what I was planning. Maybe she was afraid I'd contaminate her.

The hands released me, and I felt a firm slap to my cheek, but I only concentrated harder, my eyes still closed.

"No!" Redge shouted. I think he yanked me sideways, away from Rylant.

I felt a sharp blow on the top of my head, and I fell to the floor, smacking my elbow and the back of my head. Rainbow pinwheels of pain flowered in my mind.

How pretty, I thought, and let the pain wash through me.

"Lenni, are you all right?" I heard Redge ask.

I inhaled deeply, wishing I could inhale Mur's scent – the dark undergrowth of the forest, rich with promise. But I told myself she was still with me, cheering me on.

"Doctor Frank, I order you to stop her!" Rylant's voice was high, almost hysterical.

"But . . . how?" Doctor Frank's voice trembled.

Then I heard nothing more, except for the sound of the rushing wind. Somehow, I had become a torrent of howling fury. I was spinning into a cyclone, speeding toward Rylant's energy with more force than I thought possible.

I could sense an immense presence ahead but could see only shadow. Swirling into a furious storm, I had an inkling of the vast energy of the universe. Then the presence loomed large – an enormous sphere made of iron or steel with millions of protruding spikes aimed at me. Could this be Rylant's defenses?

It was too large, too massive, to tackle. Still, I hurtled closer at the same breakneck speed. Then I realized that the sphere was traveling toward me on a collision course.

I'm going to hit! I shrieked, as tiny metal darts began to shoot out from the spikes, right at me.

The wind that contained me never slowed. I veered and wove through the buzz of darts, dodging sideways as they whooshed past, barely missing me.

I couldn't survive this for long. Couldn't get through. Couldn't win. It was impossible.

Yet I plunged closer to the sphere, until I could see the rivets that pressed the giant metal plates together.

I was going to crash into the side. How would that help? I tried to slow myself – to reverse course – then suddenly realized that I had to do this thing. I had to break through Rylant's defenses. Even if it broke me.

Only the wind shrieked now. I braced myself for impact. I was aimed at a seam between two metal plates. Joints were weakest. Had to break through. For Redge. For me. For every skidge left hiding in Dawn. Rylant had to be stopped.

Good-bye, I said, maybe to myself, maybe to everything I'd known.

Then the impact came.

Like a star exploding in my mind, the pain so intense, so deep, that all my atoms must have flashed apart into a billion scurrying dots of light, scrambling to reassemble themselves in the right order. So destructive that it became sweet. To taste nothing, to be nothing, was freedom itself – and the worst loneliness of all.

I floated as a solitary mass of energy. If I had to give up everything to stop Rylant, it would be worth it. But I couldn't hope to know what had happened to Rylant then. I could only hope to re-form myself. Slowly, I began accumulating atoms, rebuilding, refocusing.

Bit by bit, I could sense again. Hear sobbing. See a tiny girl with light brown hair, her head down, her arms wrapped around her knees, shaking. Scared and alone. Rylant?

I tried to take her hand. She leaped up, jerking away from me, tears washing clean streaks down her cheeks. *You did this!* She accused me with all the poison she had.

Why do you fight? I reached again for her, trying to calm her.

To protect myself from people like you. She glowered, not letting me touch her.

I've done nothing to you.

You call this nothing? She gestured at the shards of metal that lay scattered around us, the remains of her defenses.

I stepped closer. *I'm not the enemy. You invented the enemy to scare yourself.*

I'm not scared. She paced back and forth like a trapped animal looking for an escape route.

Then prove it. I offered her my hand.

Never. She drew back, raising an arm in protection. *Get out of here.*

Please, I begged. I had to make her understand. We were not monsters – Redge and I. We were the same as her.

I said get out! Her face white with fury, she picked up a spike from her broken barricade and charged at me.

I jumped to the side, but her shoulder caught me in the chest, pushing me so hard that I flew backward.

She screamed when we touched, as if she were being burned. I flailed helplessly in the dead air, trying to get back to her.

Please, let me explain! I called, still falling endlessly backward, but her screams shattered my words before they could reach her.

I tried to swim, to glide, to twist toward her, but nothing could stop my reverse flight. Falling, tumbling, I was expelled from Rylant's world, her energy body. How could such a little girl be so strong?

"Lenni! Lenni!" Someone was shouting my name. Calling me back from the wind, the darkness, the abyss. A woman's voice, bringing me home.

I opened my eyes. The harsh florescent lights in the hall of the medical unit were blinding. Heads made a circle around me. Doctor Frank, Redge, and Elyle. How did she get here? Rylant must have released her. I felt a smile widen my lips. Elyle was safe.

I raised my head, looking for Rylant. Sat up, strong. "Where's Rylant?"

Elyle hugged me around the shoulders. "Oh, Lenni! I thought you were . . ."

"I'm fine," I said, glad to be hugging her back. I'd had no seizure, no dizziness. "But how's Rylant?"

Redge was grinning, his eyes wide in amazement. "She's over there."

Then I saw Doctor Frank move to examine Rylant, who sat propped up against the wall. Her eyes were wandering, her half-smile vacant. I could see the little girl in her, in the innocence of her gaze as she struggled to focus on me.

When she finally recognized me, her face changed, contorted in agony, a tormented grimace, her eyes dark with pain.

"What have I done?" she moaned. Then she let out a strangled cry.

the cabal

Healing held a terrifying power – like holding the sun in your hands without getting burned. It was unwieldy. It begged to corrupt. But there were boundaries that shouldn't be crossed.

"I think she'll be all right," Doctor Frank was saying, as Rylant began to sob into his chest. "You'd better get going, Lenni."

There's a difference between healing people and bending them to your will. At least that was what I told myself. Rylant had been sick with prejudice, conditioned to fear and hate.

"If only I'd known . . ." Rylant sniveled, her haunted eyes finding me over Doctor Frank's shoulder. "I shouldn't have . . ."

Guilt was consuming her. Guilt for what she'd done to others. It might be hard for her to face, but she'd made her own decisions.

"Where are you going?" Elyle turned to me, apprehension in her eyes.

I think she knew my answer before I said it. How could I stay in Dawn with everything that had happened? Still, it was hard to speak the words. As gently as I could, I explained about my reclassification, how Doctor Frank had found someone to help me relocate, and how Rylant had tried to stop me. I told her how glad I was that Rylant had released her and how I had healed Mother and found sketching again, without Mur's help. And I thanked her for telling me the truth about my father. "I'm so glad to have you as family," I said.

Doctor Frank scratched at his rash. "You can't stay here. More guards will be along soon." He nodded at Rylant, who was still moaning softly. "She would have notified others."

More guards. My breath caught in my throat. Could Rylant call them off? No. Rylant was just one wheel in the massive machine that was Purity. New guards would always be ready to replace her. I had to get away.

Elyle sighed heavily. "I'd hoped we could be together, have a chance to talk. There's so much to say."

I scrunched my eyes closed for a moment. How could I make this right with Elyle? How could I explain this quickly?

I tried again, my chest aching as I found Elyle's wounded eyes. "For so long, I kept all the things I knew about Mur, about drawing, inside. It was hard to pretend to fit in, to ignore who I was. And lonely, too." I held Elyle's hands. "Then, when I healed you, everything got worse. People looked at me differently. Some were afraid. Others hated me. Now, I have a chance to find a place where I can belong. I have to go, Elyle."

Elyle's injured look brought tears to my eyes.

"You're just so . . . young, so inexperienced." She shook her head. "But I want you to be safe, to live well."

"Hurry up." Doctor Frank's voice was urgent. "We'll be discovered soon."

"But your parents!" Elyle gripped my arm. "You need to see them . . . ."

"There's no more time!" Redge said.

I glanced at Redge and Doctor Frank, silencing them both. I had to get away, but without regrets. "Elyle, please tell Mother and Dad . . . tell them that . . ." That I understood now why they'd engineered me? Offered the myth of perfection, who could resist? Yet it was just a myth, one that mislead, tormented, and destroyed. A mirage that vanished the closer you got to it. "Tell them that I'm all right."

Elyle nodded, her face pale and pinched. Then she embraced me, without saying a word. I could feel her chest rising and falling, her breath on my neck. Until I finally pulled away to see Doctor Frank glancing nervously down the hall.

"I'm going now." I swallowed hard.

"I'm going, too." Redge swung his wheelchair to face Doctor Frank, jutting his chin out defiantly.

"What?" I said, surprised.

"No, Redge," Doctor Frank pleaded. "Stay with me. We need to finish those procedures."

"I don't want the procedures, Doc." Redge's face was deadly serious. "I can't be disappointed by you again. I'm leaving with Lenni."

"Redge, please." Doctor Frank kneeled on the floor in front of Redge and gripped his hand. "If you left, well . . . it would be like losing a son."

I was stunned.

"Maybe you consider me a son, but you're no father to me. I'm going, Doc, and you can't stop me." Redge wheeled backward away from Doctor Frank, leaving him kneeling pathetically alone.

"Redge!" Elyle scolded him.

I didn't know what to say. Doctor Frank was devastated, but it was Redge's decision.

"As . . . you . . . wish." Doctor Frank could hardly speak. His face blanched white as he stood up, shaking. "Good luck, Lenni. Good-bye, Redge."

"Bye, Doc." The hard edge was gone from Redge's voice. He sounded almost jubilant as he looked toward the elevator.

"Thank you, Doctor," I said. "For everything."

"Go. And take good care." Doctor Frank turned back to Rylant. I don't think he could bear to watch Redge leave.

"We will."

I felt Elyle's eyes on my back as we hurried down the hall. Without another word, Redge and I entered the elevator. Redge slammed a button on the panel, and the doors clanged shut with a terrible echo, leaving me with the memory of Elyle's forlorn face.

On the first floor, we rushed down a quiet corridor toward the back courtyard. My stomach was fluttering and I was breathing hard. Only once was I sure that we would be stopped – when we almost ran into two Purity guards. But we hid in an open doorway, held our breath until they passed, then moved on. By the time we got to the courtyard exit, I was ready to burst through the door and keep running. But it was locked.

"Hurry!" I hissed, as Dawg retrieved the security code.

Redge typed it into the computer panel beside the door, his fingers fumbling. After seconds that lasted lifetimes, the heavy metal door clicked open.

I went first, stepping into the courtyard, and breathing in the humid air of freedom. Redge followed.

"Where is she?" I turned in a circle, taking in the garden, winding stone paths, high fence, and gate.

The scent of rain was in the air, and the glorious fragrance of leaves. I'd never seen this garden before from the windows or the street beyond. It was astoundingly peaceful. An oasis.

"We're here." I turned at the sound of Duke's voice.

Duke and Rae emerged from behind some dense bushes. Rae's gray-black hair swept down over her shoulders to the middle of her back. She stepped lightly, even with a large pack on her back. Duke was dressed all in black.

"I thought we were only collecting one." Duke winked at Rae, his ponytail swinging. "But I guess we could find a use for one more."

"I suppose so," Rae agreed. She passed me some moss-green coveralls that the forest patrol wear. "Here, put these on over your gown." She also handed me some shoes.

It was real. I was going to get out of Dawn, get away from Purity. I hurried into the clothes, rejoicing to wear something other than that hateful hospital gown. Relief broke over me in waves, washing away the fear, the terror, and the hurt of the last few weeks. I was going to make it. I would be free.

Redge grinned. "You know, Duke, all that talk in the cafeteria – it's hardly a good cover."

"Sometimes the best disguise is the truth," Rae arched an eyebrow.

Duke snorted. Then he laughed.

And, even though I had no idea where I was going or what would happen next, I smiled, too.

toward the sun

I tramped through the forest, matching Rae's bouncing stride, dizzy with the pleasure of branches whispering, leaves brushing my arms, the late-afternoon sun dodging rain clouds, and the vast sky. With every step, I was lighter, calmer, more invigorated.

Behind me, Redge struggled happily along on a pair of quickly fashioned, tree-branch crutches. Duke followed, lugging Redge's wheelchair on his back. Redge wouldn't allow himself to be carried.

My feet moved in a steady rhythm. My eyes flicked from the roots and stones hidden in shadows on the forest floor to the reassuring presence of the pack on Rae's solid back. A mix of mushroom and spruce tickled my nose, bringing back bittersweet memories of Mur. And here and there, lifewort waved its serrated leaves. It had overrun the forest, too, and I hoped Dad would find a way to contain and reinvent it in a new, less invasive way. I wouldn't want it to destroy the forest.

We went uphill, circling branches, trying to avoid leaving tracks. I kept expecting to come to the perimeter fence that surrounded Dawn, the fence that enclosed the city, the lake, and a huge area of forest. We had traveled so far, yet we were still inside.

Then I heard the roar of the waterfall and I knew where we were – on the ridge across the lake from Dawn, below the hydro unit. If I broke from the shadowy forest and found an outcrop of rock, I would see across the lake to Dawn, nestled peacefully between the hills. But what went on there was far from peaceful.

Rae stopped us by the edge of the waterfall. "We'll rest here for a bit. Get organized."

The thunder of the waterfall pounded in my chest. A soothing spray coated my arms and face. My leg muscles twitched after the long hike. Redge dropped onto a mossy log, set his crutches beside him, and rubbed under one arm where the crutches had held him.

Duke lowered Redge's wheelchair to the ground. "Welcome to Cabal Headquarters!" He gestured energetically at the wide-open sky and the clusters of aspen and fir.

"So the cabal is real?" Redge asked, looking at Duke eagerly.

"You bet it is," Duke said.

Then, as if he hadn't just hiked all the way from Dawn with Redge's chair on his back, he marched over to the waterfall and inhaled deeply.

"Duke would like to think it's real," Rae said, opening her pack, "but it's mostly talk."

Duke turned with a grunt. "Rae doesn't have the full vision." His tone was light, but I got the sense he was serious. "We should be doing more to fight Purity. I've been working on plans."

"Destruction isn't going to bring about public enlightenment, Duke." Rae passed around a large canteen of water. "What did the sabotage of the solar grid achieve?"

"You did that?" Redge was staring, amazed, at Duke.

I wasn't impressed.

"Yes, he did," Rae jumped in before Duke could answer. Yet it was clear from his grin that Duke had done it and he was proud. Rae continued, "But we've also been writing and distributing articles, under pseudonyms, that promote acceptance."

"Come on, Rae," Duke said. "We've got to do more than that! Purity is worldwide! We need to fight for rights for the genetic underclass. We need to destroy Purity. We need to create an army!"

I took a long gulp from the canteen. I knew I'd always resist Purity with all I had. Not like Duke wanted to, with violence and sabotage, but in my own way — helping one person at a time.

"You're a master of words, Duke," Rae was smiling and shaking her head. "They're a powerful tool. But we've had this conversation before. I'm here to help people. I'm not prepared to go to war."

"What *do* you do?" I asked Rae, hoping to stop the argument.

"I operate an underground escape service for those who need it," she began. "Duke helps me out with that. We can get you away from Purity, give you a new identity, help you get settled. The rest is up to you."

Leave Dawn forever. I couldn't have imagined it a month ago. Now I was looking forward to it. Everything had happened so quickly. It had been only three and a half weeks since I'd first healed that woman, that stranger, down in the commons. That was when the nightmare had begun. *Are you skidge? Purity will be after you.* Inside my pocket, I rubbed my waterstone, remembering Elyle's face as the elevators doors closed. I'd left so much behind.

"That's amazing!" Two bright spots shone pink on Redge's cheeks.

Rae smiled at him. "Just my way of helping out." She pulled a small package from her pack. "How about a sustenance bar?"

"I'll have one." My stomach rumbled at the mention of food.

"Me, too," said Redge, "and I want to hear about this escape service." He grinned. "How much for a one-way ticket?"

"Yes, where will we go?" I leaned against Redge's mossy log to eat my bar. It was delicious, the best I'd ever eaten. I had to be hungry to think that.

"Right now, I'm sending folks to the far north." Rae sat beside me. "It's been warming up there fast and some new areas can now be settled. I've been working with a remote Inuit village to help people get established."

"So we're really going to the Beyond!" Redge looked like he didn't know what to think.

"It has to be better than Dawn," I told him, remembering how Rae had said she'd lived in the Beyond for years. Somehow, that helped.

Rae smiled. "It's not so bad. You may fit in better than you think." Then her face grew serious. "It's a harsh life in the north, I won't kid you. The land is going through a terrible time as the earth warms, but the people are supportive and it would be your life to make."

Redge looked skeptical, but he nodded.

"That's enough chatting." Rae stood. "Redge, I know you've scrambled Purity's link to your monitor. We can't remove it for you, but Duke is going to disengage it permanently. We don't want you found again. And I'm going to organize the supplies you'll need before we go beyond the fence."

She began to rummage through her pack again, handing Duke a strange metal device shaped like a prong. Duke took it, then began to use it against the side of Redge's neck, just behind his ear.

"I can't wait to be free of this," Redge said.

"Stay still then." Duke gave him a friendly smack on the side of his head.

Into the Beyond. What would I find there? How would I live? I had so many questions, but I knew I had to trust Rae and be ready for anything.

"You need one of these?" Rae handed me a slate and stylus. Of course, Redge had brought his own slate, with Dawg safely in it.

"Thanks!" I took the slate, thinking sadly of the lifetime of sketches I'd left behind. Well, I would have to start again. I hoped that where I was going my art would be better received than it had been in Dawn.

The slate was an older model. Nothing like the sleek, modern one I'd left at the medical unit. Still, I liked the familiar weight of it in my hands.

"It's a clunker, but it'll do," Rae shrugged. "And you'll need these clothes and supplies." She was making a pile beside me. "I'll put together a pack for you to carry."

Then Duke was stuffing the tool back into Rae's pack, while Redge was cheerfully rubbing the side of his neck, disengaged from his monitor for good. We were leaving Purity behind.

"Hey, how about a sketch of me?" Redge asked, after he'd thanked Duke about a hundred times.

I examined Redge's face, wondering what he was really asking. Would I sketch him, or would I heal his legs? But I knew the real question. *Should* I heal him? I'd had enough of fighting against nature. I had to work with it, instead.

Redge caught my intense look and returned it. His eyes flickered down to his legs then back to me. His brow was furrowed.

I knew I could help Redge and others. I'd mastered my gift, and my curse. I was powerful and dangerous. I'd become an interpreter of another plane, another level of existence. That, too, was what the water-stone meant. The figure was reaching out with both hands and connecting two worlds. But Redge wasn't broken – I understood that now – and neither was I.

A shiver ran through me. Redge stared at me, his eyes larger than I'd seen them. Rae glanced at Duke. No one spoke. Only the wind dared to whistle, the trees to creak, the waterfall to roar, and the mosquitoes to buzz nearby.

"Just a sketch," Redge said finally, his voice firm, his eyes locked on mine.

"Really?" My voice came out surprisingly fragile. I didn't want to say no to Redge. How would I explain that I didn't need to heal him? But I didn't have to say anything. Somehow, Redge knew it, too.

"Really." Redge nodded. "I've had enough of trying to be what I'm not. I just wanted to give you something to draw."

"Sure." I let out a breath. "Let me just play with this slate for a minute to get used to it."

Redge used his arms to lift and turn his body toward me. I fiddled with the slate – powered it on and began to experiment with the stylus. I sketched the rough outline of a figure running. The lines were slightly jagged, but it would do.

The strange thing was that I agreed with Purity in a way. Everyone had the right to a genetic heritage that hadn't been tampered with. Humans were good enough as we were. Higher intelligence, improved muscular ability – these shouldn't be the goals. Because more didn't always mean better.

I thought again about my waterstone. Spirit shaping, Elyle had called it. How had Elyle known so much about me, when she'd made the stone? Could she shape me? Could anyone? I thought about how Rylant had made me scared, then made me angry, then made me strong. She had shaped me, just as I had shaped her. So had

Mother and Dad. And Elyle, Jonah, Redge, Rae, Doctor Frank, and especially Mur. They had all shaped me, but they didn't make decisions for me. Not anymore.

I sketched Redge with my eyes open. His thin legs tucked sideways against the log. His muscular arms, still gleaming from the effort of the climb. His crooked grin, mischievous eyes, and proud chin. My hand flew over the slate, and I remembered sketching portraits for the simple satisfaction of capturing a person in an instant in time. Redge would never be here again, beside the waterfall, with branches waving behind his head at this moment of escape from Dawn. But I would help him remember this triumph and contentment. I would give him the visual.

When I was done, I held out my slate to Redge. Rae and Duke looked on. Redge's smile deepened as he gazed at his own image.

"There's no stopping us now," Redge yelped, slapping a hand down on his thigh.

"Not too loud," Rae cautioned.

Just then, the last of the day's sun broke through the cloud, filtered through the leaves, and warmed me. The rocks that lined the waterfall sparkled where the sun struck them, as if someone had scattered tiny jewels. I smiled.

"We don't need to worry about these two kids in the Beyond." Duke whacked me on the back too hard.

Rae nodded, her brown eyes level with mine, one eye delightfully higher and smaller than the other.

I had no idea what we would face once we were on the other side of the fence. The Beyond was a huge void to me, shaped only by stories and gossip. Maybe it would be filled with half-crazed skidge. Or maybe I'd find people like Redge and me. Either way, only I would decide who I was, what I would become. With every sketch I made. With every decision, every movement, every day.

acknowledgements

A writer may work alone day after day, but a book is the combined effort of many. During the writing of this book, Karen Rankin read the manuscript more than once with a careful eye. Many others also gave valuable feedback at various stages, including Peter Carver, Rosemary Hood, Rick Lord, Cheryl Rainfield, Trudee Romanek, and Kathy Stinson. At Second Story Press, Margie Wolfe, Laura McCurdy, and the rest of the staff offered continued support and encouragement. Editor Kathryn Cole was insightful, sensitive, and a pleasure to work with. The Canada Council for the Arts and the City of Toronto through the Toronto Arts Council provided financial support. And my family – Kevin, Paige, and Tess – endured the trials and celebrated the joys with me. Thanks to all for sharing the journey.